KILLER EYES!

Captain Gringo and Ynez passed an old baroque church with its oaken door ajar, spilling a tripwire of golden light across the cobbles. Beyond, the street bottlenecked through an archway and ran dark as a mineshaft toward a distant pinpoint of light. Ynez said that was the doorway they were headed for.

As they moved arm in arm toward the distant tiny light, it winked off and on. Ynez didn't notice. Most people wouldn't have. But most people weren't Captain Gringo. He shoved the Basque girl into a deeply recessed doorway and flattened out against her, drawing his .38, as the machinegun aimed their way opened up, filling the narrow passage with stacatto noise and flame!

Novels by Ramsay Thorne

Renegade #1
Renegade #2: Blood Runner
Renegade #3: Fear Merchant
Renegade #4: The Death Hunter
Renegade #5: Macumba Killer
Renegade #6: Panama Gunner
Renegade #7: Death in High Places
Renegade #8: Over The Andes to Hell
Renegade #9: Hell Raider
Renegade #10: The Great Game
Renegade #11: The Dreyfus Affair
Renegade #12: Badlands Brigade
Renegade #13: The Mahogany Pirates
Renegade #14: Harvest of Death
Renegade #15: Terror Trail

Published by
WARNER BOOKS

Renegade #15

TERROR TRAIL

by

Ramsay Thorne

A Warner Communications Company

WARNER BOOKS EDITION

Warner Books, Inc.,
75 Rockefeller Plaza,
New York, N.Y. 10019

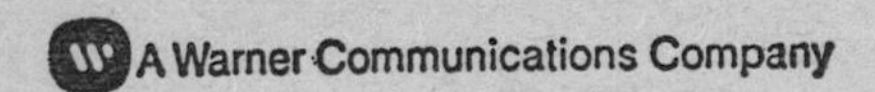

Printed in the United States of America

First Printing: November, 1982

10 9 8 7 6 5 4 3 2 1

Renegade #15

TERROR TRAIL

Roaming in the gloaming could get spooky in the tropics. As Captain Gringo strode along the nearly deserted cobbled quay, the harbor waters of Corozal lay quiet as a mill pond, reflecting the ugly sunset sky above. The setting sun to the west was a dull pumpkin pie and the sullen sky had a bad case of gangrene. Purple clouds edged with greenish mustard were moving seaward against the usual trade winds. At sea level, the air was heavy, humid, still, and smelled like the breech block of an overheated machinegun. Captain Gringo hadn't fired a machinegun in recent memory, so he knew the only other answer was a pending visit from the Great Carib Sky God, Hurikan.

He squinted out across the harbor, cursing under his breath. The native fishing boats had been hauled up on the quay as the native fishermen headed for higher ground. So where in the hell was that effing Greystoke's yacht and, more important, where was his effing *money?* Captain

Gringo and his sidekick, Gaston, hadn't hacked their way all the way down to the coast through all that spinach to admire the ugly little town of Corozal under an even uglier sunset. They'd done the job British Intelligence had hired them to do up in the highlands, and Greystoke had said he'd be waiting here with the pay-off. Unless the sardonic Englishman enjoyed putting out to sea in hurricane weather, it looked like a kiss-off instead of a pay-off!

As he moved along the quay, Captain Gringo noticed an out-of-place feminine figure seated pensively on a mooring stanchion, gazing out to sea. Even a native girl would have seemed out of place there with a hurricane about to blow over the horizon any minute. This particular addition to an otherwise dull landscape looked like she'd been drawn by Charles Dana Gibson. But Captain Gringo didn't stop to ask her what a blond Gibson Girl was doing in Corozal. It seemed logical enough to see a girl with Anglo-Saxon dress and features in a British Honduran port, once you thought about it. Her sporty middy and simple skirt indicated she was as modern a miss as the other Gibson Girls and he wasn't up to explaining the facts of Latin American life to her right now. With the quay deserted, it hardly seemed likely any local lothario would take her lack of an escort as an invitation and, what the hell, if she didn't have enough sense to head back to her hotel or whatever before those storm clouds up there burst, she deserved to get wet.

He was more interested in another figure coming down the quay to meet him: Gaston. The dapper little Frenchman had obviously completed his own sweep from the far end of the harbor when Captain Gringo stopped and took out a Havana Claro. He noticed how damp the air was when he had to thumb the match head more than once to light it.

Gaston Verrier, late of the French Foreign Legion, joined Captain Gringo to say, "*Merde alors,* we have been crossed double, Dick. I just spoke to a certain rogue I know, up at the chandler's shop near the far end of the quay. That species of an Englishman weighed anchor two days ago, while we were toiling our way through the thrice-accursed jungle!"

Captain Gringo snorted smoke out his nostrils like a bull looking for someone to gore before he replied, "So Greystoke hasn't put out to sea because of the storm warnings. Goddamn it, I knew he was going to cross us when we took the fucking job. Why do I do things like that, Gaston?"

Gaston shrugged and said, "Perhaps you have a glandular problem. To be just, Greystoke may have thought we were not coming back, hein? We were in the highlands quite some time. I warned you those extra weeks you spent with the très grateful Spanish widow might discourage our British business associates from waiting about for us, non?"

Captain Gringo grinned sheepishly and answered, "What can I tell you? She wasn't just grateful, she was great. Besides, we needed the vacation to steady our nerves after smoking up those chocolate soldiers, right?"

"I enjoyed the native girls I shacked up with, too. But enough of this ancient history, my old and horny. Obviously we are not about to be paid for the more fatiguing parts of our mission and, just as obviously, we can't linger here in British Honduras too long before some très fatigue official asks annoying questions. It's one thing to be working under the wing of an understanding British Intelligence but it's another to explain all those tedious reward posters to the colonial constabulary, non?"

Captain Gringo nodded, blew a thoughtful smoke ring, and watched it hang in the breathless brassy air as he said, "When you're right, you're right. We don't know where in hell Greystoke's gone with our money, and we probably don't have enough ready cash to follow him if we did. Do you think we have enough between us to make it back to Costa Rica?"

Gaston looked wistful and replied, "*Ordinary* passage to Limon, *oui*. The undivided loyalty of a purser who doubtless has our reward posters on his cabin bulkhead, non. We are going to have to pick up more work, somewhere closer, Dick."

Captain Gringo glanced landward with a thoughtful frown. The sun was down behind the tile roofing of Corozal now, so it would soon be dark. "The British colonial cops are a pain in the ass about guys they don't know on the streets at night," he volunteered. "The first thing we'd better think about is a place to hole up."

"*Oui,* what about the hotel we stayed in the last time we were here?"

"No good. I made some enemies at the hotel and our only friend in high places seems to have skipped out on us. Don't you know anyone in town we can trust for a night or two?"

Gaston shrugged and answered, "I know lots of people along the Mosquito Coast, Dick. As for *trusting* any of them, don't be silly. I know a semi-retired lady of the evening in Belize who would doubtless shelter us for old times' sake. She admires the way I make love and she must have a friend for you. Alas, Belize is over sixty of your Yankee miles down the coast."

Captain Gringo looked the other way: the seaward horizon was greenish black and the overhead green and purple clouds were moving faster to meet it. He said, "I don't know about you, but a sixty-mile stroll along the beach in a hurricane doesn't sound like much fun!"

"I agree. It won't be safe, here, in an hour or less. But regard that très strange English type, back there. What on earth could she have in mind?"

Captain Gringo turned and regarded the Gibson Girl as she stood poised on the edge of the stone quay, eyes closed. Gaston murmured, "She's going to jump." And Captain Gringo agreed with him, but didn't answer. There wasn't time to as he dashed back along the quay and hooked her slim waist like an express train picking up a mail bag on the fly!

"Let me go!" she sobbed as his momentum carried them both to safer ground and he steadied her on her feet. Her eyes were still closed and tears ran down her cheeks in the dim light as she weakly struggled in his arms. He shook her gently and said, "Tell me about it. I've a .38 to lend you if you have a really good reason to die. I'm not about to let any lady drown herself in that filthy water. We're just downstream from a sewer outlet."

The incongruity of his remarks opened her eyes, but she still looked unhappy as hell and insisted, "Let me go. It's my life that's been ruined. It's my right to end it any way I see fit."

"Hey, I said I'd lend you a gun. But let's talk about it first, okay?"

By this time Gaston had joined them. The girl sobbed, tried to pull away again and then, realizing the struggle was useless, buried her face against Captain Gringo's linen-clad chest and began to bawl like a baby.

He held her, patting her trembling shoulder reassuringly as he waited for her to get it all out. Gaston asked if she was pregnant or just broke. Captain Gringo shook his head warningly and muttered, "Don't pester her. She'll tell us what's eating her when she's good and ready."

"I can't," the girl sobbed. "You're sweet to try, but I'm in enough trouble as it is. They'd kill me if I told anyone else about it!"

Captain Gringo laughed gently, and asked, "Back up and think about what you just said, honey. You're not making a hell of a lot of sense."

Gaston said, "*Oui,* one who is in fear of her life has no business leaping into Caribbeans, hein?"

The pretty would-be suicide didn't think it was funny. She shuddered in Captain Gringo's arms and insisted, "There's no hope left for me. I am done for. I may still hope for a cleaner death than the one El Cazador plans for me. I have no right to involve others in my doom!"

Captain Gringo frowned over her shoulder at Gaston, who nodded and said, "*Oui,* that means The Hunter. One gathers this El Cazador, whoever he may be, takes a dramatic view of life."

"I'm Dick Walker," Captain Gringo informed the girl, "and this is Gaston Verrier and we're on your side, Miss . . . ?"

"Harlow, Morgana Harlow. Originally from Mayfair."

"I didn't take you for a señorita. Look, it's going to start raining and blowing pretty good any minute, Miss Harlow. What say we all get to high ground before we talk it over, eh?"

"I'm tired of running. I've run so far, and so far he's always caught up with me."

"Yeah. Meanwhile we're about to get blown away in a hurricane. Do you have a place of your own here in Corozal?"

She nodded and answered, "I've rented a private house, but we can't go there. I think El Cazador knows where I've been staying!"

"You *think?* Hell, things are looking up. I know for sure this quay's about to get hit with at least a twenty-foot tide any minute. We'll take our chances on a jerk-off with a gun!"

Morgana Harlow kept insisting it wasn't safe for them to take her home but they did it anyway. By the time they reached her one-story, rented house, wrapped around a small patio, the sky was black and the wind was howling like hungry wolves. At ground level the air was going the other way, picking up trash and dust and spitting big gobs of warm rain ahead of it. The house was on a hillside Captain Gringo hoped was high enough. The stout oaken gate was barred on the inside and they had to pound a while before a frightened looking housekeeper opened up for them. As they ducked in and locked the gate behind them, again the chica sobbed, "Oh, señorita, I was so worried about you. I fear we are about to have a most terrible storm!"

The English girl was still confused. So Captain Gringo asked the native girl if there were any other servants and if anyone had come calling on La Señorita while she was out. The chica shook her head and said, "No to both questions, señor. I was so frightened at the thought of spending the night here all alone! Forgive me, I am trying to be brave, but when I was little, a hurricane swept through my home village and many of my people died. Do you think we shall die, here, tonight?"

It was a good question. Captain Gringo smiled reassuringly and said, "We're behind stout walls on high ground. But we could all wind up with the ague if we don't see about drying things out a bit. Which way is the room with the biggest fireplace? I don't usually take charge this way, but you can see your señorita is not herself this evening."

The chica nodded and led them around the patio arcade to a drawing room whose walls were thick stucco, and the furnishings were spartan. But the room was cozy, for the little housekeeper had already kindled a blaze in the baronial baroque plaster fireplace. There was no other illumination and the flames were acting funny as the wind above whipped across the flue. As he sat the lady of the house down on a leather sofa near the fire, Captain Gringo noticed the native girl wasn't bad, either. She was maybe half Indian with various white and Negro genes making up the difference to give her that oddly raceless, exotic look you saw down here in bananaland. She was a little plump for Captain Gringo's taste. Gaston took her arm as he asked her if she'd started fires in the other rooms and, if she hadn't, offered to help. Captain Gringo didn't comment as the sly old dog left with the pretty little wench. Morgana Harlow seemed not to notice or, if she noticed, not to care. She sat upright, tensely staring into the flickering flames as if she saw something there that made her nervous as hell.

Captain Gringo sat beside her, placing his planter's hat on the end table and opening his jacket to leave the grip of his shoulder holstered .38 free for any action that might arise. He asked, "Is it all right for me to smoke, ma'am?" and the English girl nodded but said, "You must leave as soon as you finish one cigar. You and Gaston are in terrible danger here."

He struck a light and got his claro going before he answered calmly, "You're wrong. Aside from a hurricane blowing outside, Gaston and I have guys hunting for us, too. If I tell you my story, will you tell me yours?"

She didn't answer. He blew a cloud of smoke at the fire, nodded, and said, "I'll make it short and sweet. I used to be a U.S. Army officer until I got in trouble. They court martialed me and sentenced me to hang—up in the States. I didn't like the idea too much. I had to kill a good-for-nothing fellow officer as I escaped from the guard house. I jumped the border and met up with Gaston in a Mexican jail. The Mexicans wanted to execute us both although we've never quite figured out why. We smoked up a mess of guys as we escaped from there, too. Since then we've been knocking around Latin America, doing odd jobs for people. We're what that reporter, Richard Harding Davis, likes to call 'soldiers of fortune.' In other words, we fight people for a living or, sometimes, just to keep on living. I'm a trained machinegunner and a fairly good all-around gunfighter. Gaston's older and shorter, but he's fairly good in a scrap, too. We're on your side because, frankly, it's the only offer we've had all day. We need a place to hole up and you obviously need somebody to protect you. Do we have a deal?"

She sighed and answered, "I don't seem to have much choice. I told you not to meddle in my affairs. But you insisted, and if El Cazador's men have spotted you two gallant fools in my company—and they probably have—he has you and Gaston on his death list too, now!"

"Okay, I'll just put the son-of-a-bitch on *my* list, as soon as you tell me who on earth we're talking about. Who, or what, is El Cazador?"

She grimaced and replied, "Among other things, he's my husband. At least, he's my *legal* husband. I don't suppose you'd believe me if I told you the marriage was never consummated?"

He leaned back and stared thoughtfully at her. Morgana's cameo profile was turned to him, so he could examine her at leisure: she looked pretty good. Aside from having a beautiful face, her modern attitude about corsetage and her thin damp middy blouse revealed a figure that made one doubt the sanity of any man married to such a dish in name only. That twenty-two or -three inch waistline was real, not whalebone, and he made her about thirty-six, firm, around the chest.

She apparently took his polite silence for disbelief, for she said, "It wasn't my idea. I'll confess I didn't come to my marriage quite a virgin. I didn't love Roderico when I married him in London a few months ago. But I married him in good faith and I would have been willing to play my part as the wife of a reasonably attractive man with, well, a lot of money."

"Is that why you married the guy?"

"Yes. I told him so from the beginning. You see, he started paying court to me as I was breaking up with a former lover who hadn't treated me very nicely, either."

She suddenly blushed and said, "Oh, dear, all this raking over old embers does make me look a bit low, doesn't it?"

He shrugged and said, "If you were really low, you wouldn't feel low. I just got through telling you I'm wanted in the States for murder and I feel fine about *my* conscience. But leaving value judgment aside, you're confusing me pretty good. Why don't you just start at the beginning? I'll shoot anybody who busts in to interrupt your tale."

Morgana turned to him with a sad little smile and said, "I thnk you would, but El Cazador is very dangerous and . . ."

"Let me be the judge of that," he interrupted, adding, "First of all, you have to tell me who the hell he is and why you call him some macho nickname when he's still your darling hubby, Roderico, on paper."

She nodded and explained, "I didn't know he was El Cazador when we met in London. Now that I do know, I can't think of him as anything else."

"The beginning, Babe. Start at the beginning."

She looked away, cheeks flushed, as she said softly, "That's the hard part. My story is all too familiar. It starts with an innocent Essex country girl who'd been told, too often, she was the prettiest young thing in a sleepy English village. She could have had her pick of the honest rustic lads she met at the grange dances, but she thought she was too pretty."

"Gotcha. Let me guess at the next chapter. She went to London to be an actress, a model, or something, right?"

"Close enough. I wound up the mistress of a handsome playboy with a grand house in Mayfair, a title and, well, a wife. I know that sounds dreadfully sordid, Dick, but I *was* in love with him and he *did* make certain promises and . . ."

"And you were a country girl. You don't have to explain how you got into the fix. How did you get out?"

"I walked out. I lived in luxurious sin for about a year before I realized my lover had no intention of keeping his promises to me. I'd made friends in Mayfair. I told you he had a title. I thought I could be accepted socially without him. I suppose, in a way, I was. There were ever so many men who wanted to be my friend, on the same terms. None of them offered more honorable terms, until Roderico Montalban met me at a posh party. He was introduced to me as a wealthy Central American planter who'd just been to Africa, on safari, with some English friends. He seemed to be smitten with me at first sight. He proposed a few days later. I told him I didn't love him but he said it didn't matter, that he'd attended college in England and had always meant to have an English wife. Some rot about Hispanic women being too possessive, I think. Frankly, I wasn't paying much attention at first. Then, with both my married ex-lover and bill collectors badgering me . . ."

"Gotcha. You jumped from the frying pan into the fire. You married this weird latin and came down here with him to, where . . . ?"

"Quintana Roo. That's his headquarters. Actually he says he has land holdings all over Central America. but his home hacienda is on the coast of Quintana Roo. There's hardly another living soul for miles all around."

Captain Gringo nodded and agreed, "You can say that again. I know that part of Mexico, the hard way. "It's a territory, not a state, because it's just about empty unless you count the monkeys and the parrots in the jungle up that way. Is that why you ran away, because it was so lonely?"

She shook her head and said, "No. The hacienda itself was quite luxurious, as a matter of fact, and my husband didn't mistreat me. He didn't even seem to want to *sleep* with me when he was home, and he was . . . away a lot."

Captain Gringo thought he was getting the picture, now. He nodded and said, "Okay, so you got bored and sort of horny. So you wanted out. Only, old Roderico was one of those old-fashioned Spanish Grandees who look on a wife as property and when you ditched him for somebody younger and prettier . . ."

"I swear no other man was involved!" she cut in, adding, "I haven't been with any man since I left my English lover, and that was nearly a year ago! I left on my own, while El Cazador was out—hunting. That was why I left him, Dick. I just couldn't live with a man who lived for *hunting*, as he called it."

Captain Gringo frowned and said, "Well, it sounds kind of picky, since you knew when you met the guy that he liked to hunt. Lots of aristocratic types enjoy hunting to the point of boredom for their wives but . . ."

"You don't understand, Dick," she cut in, "my husband doesn't hunt the way other men hunt. He says he finds it banal to track down mere beasts, since a crack shot with a human brain has too much of an advantage over any animal . . . except one."

Captain Gringo frowned at her and said, "You're kidding!"

But she sobbed, "I wish to God I were, Dick, but it's true. They call him El Cazador because he lives only to hunt, and he only hunts *people!*"

Captain Gringo didn't answer. Outside, the wind was really picking up. The flames in the grate danced like hell fires and, come to think of it, the dame he was sitting with was pretty spooky, too!

Her voice was bleak as she went on: "He didn't go to Africa to shoot lions, Dick. He was with a British colonial expedition into cannibal country. They sent him home, under a cloud. I later learned why. It seems even our rougher colonials have certain sporting rules, and one is not supposed to shoot even a cannibal unless the chap makes some sort of threatening gesture. It gets worse. When he left me to go hunting in the Mexican lowland jungles, he naturally didn't find any cannibals but he found simple Indians and peasants. He shot them. He calls that hunting, you see."

Captain Gringo whistled softly and said, "Wow, that's a bit rich, even for Mexico under Diaz! Does the Mexican government know about El Cazador's odd hobby, Morgana?"

"I don't know about the central government. We frequently entertained the chief of the local Rurales who seemed to feel he was a fine fellow. I know for a fact that some of his Mexican friends have joined him on his little hunting expeditions. Don't ask me why."

"I don't have to: most Hispanics enjoy blood sports more than we do, and you have to be a real bastard to work for El Presidente Diaz. Okay, I get the picture. You married a maniac. Now you've run away from him and you think he's after you. Get to the good part. Why do you think he's still tracking you, Morgana?"

"Two reasons. We're not that far from the Mexican border and this afternoon, when I went to see about a steamer ticket home, I saw one of my husband's trackers loitering around the steamship office."

"Ouch! Okay, you had enough sense to take some money along. These walls are almost a yard thick, even if they know you rented this house. So, next question, what are the odds they know about this place?"

She shrugged and said, "If El Cazador doesn't know this address at the moment, he soon will. I'm sure the servant at the steamship office spotted me this afternoon. This is a small town. How many Anglo-Saxon women could have rented a room or anything else here in Corozal?"

Captain Gringo nodded and said, "Yeah, they've been known to gossip about *me* in the market place, too. Sit tight. I've got to check a few details before we make any plans."

She asked where he was going as he rose and walked to the door. It was too dumb a question to answer, so he didn't. It was black as pitch and howling like a banshee outside. Striking a light was out of the question as the wind whipped around the patio like God was using it for a police whistle. But fortunately the layout of the house was simple. The rooms were strung like beads on a string around the patio. All doors and windows opened on the wrap-around arcade. So the tall American just groped his way toward the main entrance, feeling his way from one post to the next. Though he was under the arcade's overhang, he was quickly soaked from the waist down by the wind-whipped rain. He yelled for Gaston a couple of times before the Frenchman's voice called back, "Over here, my rude and noisy youth. One hopes you had a good reason for putting me in this most ridiculous upright posture, hein?"

As Captain Gringo got close enough to see Gaston dimly outlined by the lamp light from the open doorway behind him, he saw what the Frenchman meant. Gaston was naked as a jay, save for the .38 in his fist. As the taller American became more visible Gaston snorted in disgust and said, "*Merde alors,* why are you still dressed? Did not I leave you with the best-looking woman in the place?"

"We haven't had a chance to talk about that, yet," Captain Gringo replied, then quickly filled Gaston in on El Cazador's odd hobby and asked if Gaston had any suggestions.

Gaston waved his free hand out at the whirling gale taking up most of the patio space as he said, "We will drown if we go out in that hurricane. Morgana's tedious husband will drown if *he* goes out in it, too."

"Maybe, but she says he's *nuts,* and I believe her. We have to check out the security here, Gaston."

"*Merde alors,* do you take me for a fool, my worried youth? I, Gaston, never remove my pants without taking certain precautions. As I was, ah, getting to know the housekeeper I had her show me about the premises. Pepita's room, as you can see, is right next to the only entrance to the street and the gate is barred on the inside. Perhaps a battering ram would serve to open it, but one imagines Pepita and I would hear it, no matter who was on top at the moment. There are no windows facing the outside—only one wall faces the street. The other three are well secured by other houses."

"Okay, what if some son-of-a-bitch decides to crawl over the roofs at us?"

"In a hurricane? Aside from having the wind literally up his ass, he would make *le crunch crunch* on the fragile roof tiles, non?"

Captain Gringo nodded. This house and the ones around it were single story and crudely built with the tiles layed over exposed ceiling beams and rafters. He said, "Okay, we seem to be forted up good for the moment. Even a maniac would be nuts to charge in blind against two armed men in the dark. If neither of us heard him coming over the roof he has no way of even guessing which room either of us are in."

"Do you think we should, ah, hole up closer together, Dick?"

"No. Aside from embarrassing Morgana, I just said it was better for us to be spread out so that he can't crash in on one of us without the other shooting him in the ass. You know the sound of my .38 and I won't be smashing any wood. So if you hear anybody else doing it, aim low and roll away from your flash."

Gaston snorted in disgust and said, "I was gunfighting in the dark before you were born. I grasp our simple plan of operations, Dick. Now, if you will forgive me, I must return to the French lesson I was giving Pepita. I am pleased to say she seems a willing pupil, despite her lack of experience."

"Kiss it once for me," Captain Gringo laughed, and headed back to where he'd left Morgana. The English girl was crouched behind a chest in a far corner as he came in.

"Oh," she gasped, "I was so frightened, Dick! Why did you rush out like that? Did you hear something?"

"No," he said. "I was making sure I would. Where's your bedroom, Morgana?"

"I beg your pardon?"

"Relax. We're not going there. Anybody planning to invade this house would be likely to ask whoever told them you were here the layout. At this hour they'd naturally expect you to be in bed, see?"

She nodded and said, "The master bedroom is up at the corner. The door faces the patio at right angles to the one behind you."

"Good. It's even better than I'd hoped. Hang on, I'll be right back."

He went out again and groped his way to the door she'd mentioned. The wind was really getting wild now and he had a struggle closing the door after him once he was in Morgana's room. He struck a match, found an oil lamp near her four poster, and lit the wick. He trimmed the lamp to a barely visible glow, cast a wistful glance at the cushy-looking feather mattress nobody was going to get to use tonight, and closed the jalousies across the glass of the closed window facing the patio. Then he hauled a chair over by the door and, with some juggling, managed to work his way outside in a way that left the chair perched upside down and ready to crash to the tile floor should anyone open said door uninvited.

He went back to Morgana in the drawing room and told

her, "Okay, we have a decoy light in your room and it's booby-trapped for noise. I'll bar this door, here, and then we'd better put out the fire."

"Won't that leave us in the dark?"

"That's the idea. It's warm enough in here and I don't want anybody even thinking about this window facing the patio. Frankly, I don't think anyone's likely to hit us tonight. But let's make 'em work at it if they do!"

After locking the door and bracing a chair under the knob, he knelt to scatter the fire coals as he explained how Gaston had the main entrance covered, leaving out the more intimate details. But as the dying embers plunged them into total darkness Morgana asked, "Are you saying Gaston means to spend the night in Pepita's room across the way?"

He allowed himself an invisible grin as he answered, "Don't worry. Gaston won't do anything to a lady she doesn't want him to."

"I'm not sure Pepita doesn't want him to. She seems a rather forward little thing."

"Yeah, well, that's their problem," said Captain Gringo, rejoining her on the big sofa as he struck another light to get his damp claro going again. She could see him well enough by the flickering match light to say, "Good Lord, you're soaking wet and we have no fire, now."

"I noticed but it can't be helped. I'll risk a head cold before a bullet in the head any night. Forget my wet duds. We've got to do some serious planning between now and morning. How much money do you have on you?"

"About six hundred pounds, why?"

"That's over a thousand U.S. dollars. Gaston and me have nearly another thousand between us. Okay, we have the wherewithal to make it down the coast to Belize, if and when this storm lets up. I'll warn you up front that it's a long soggy hike, even in the dry season. Do you walk well?"

She shuddered and answered, "I'd walk barefoot through a hundred miles of broken glass before I'd let my husband take me alive, Dick. He won't just kill me if he gets his hands on me, you know."

"Yeah, I got the part about his being sort of surly. He may or may not have trailed you this far. If we can machete our way to Belize, you'll be over sixty miles further from the Mexican border, and despite what they say about British colonial policy, the local constabulary can't be bought and Queen Victoria hangs people for murder in her colonies. To be doubly safe, once we make it to the next port of call, Gaston can slip in to town and buy you a steamboat ride while the two of us stay hidden. You don't think he'd follow you to London, do you?"

"I don't know," she sighed. "If he does, he won't find me there. I never told him of the little Essex village I grew up in. I used to be ashamed of being a farmer's daughter."

"Gotcha. Which of the rustic lads back home do you expect to settle down with, Morgana?"

"Probably the first one who asks me, unless he's deformed. I've learned my lesson, Dick. There are worse fates than a quiet life in a little English village. Milly Hanks has had all the adventure she ever bargained for!"

"I didn't hear that," he said. "I thought Morgana Harlow sounded like a made-up stage-name. But let's keep it 'til you get home and fade into the thatch of Essex. Don't tell anyone your real name until you get off the train in your own safe little part of the world, right?"

She placed a hand on his wrist, saying, "You're very understanding and very dear, Dick." Then she added, "Heavens, your flesh is cold as ice! You must be chilled to the very bone!"

"What can I tell you? That's the trouble with the tropics. When you're not too hot you're too cold. I'm okay. Like I said, I've been knocking around down here a while. The only thing anyone can do about the lousy climate is to ignore it. By this time tomorrow night we may be sweating like pigs."

"I know. I told you I've been living just up the coast for a while. But, meanwhile, you're going to catch your death if we don't do something to warm you up."

He repressed a shiver as he asked, "What have you got in mind? We can't light the fire again, damn it."

"I know," she said, "but there's still a glow of warmth from the hearth. You could feel it if you got out of those wet clothes."

"Yeah, but I haven't anything else to put on."

"What's the difference, Dick? I can't see you." She laughed and added, "We could both be sitting here stark naked without anyone noticing a thing wrong, you know."

"It might not *look* wrong," he chuckled, "but it sure would *feel* grotesque. I'm trying to be a gentleman, Morgana, but there are certain limits to my will power and, well, I've been out in the jungle for a couple of weeks with no feminine companionship—if you know what I mean."

"Oh, I know all too well what you mean," she sighed. "I've been sleeping alone even longer."

Captain Gringo didn't say another word as he stood up and started peeling off his wet duds. Morgana didn't speak either, but he could hear the rustle of her drier garments as she took them off. He put his .38 on the end table with his hat and turned around to reach out to her in the dark. She met him standing naked, and as he took her in his arms he didn't need any light to tell him how beautiful her body was. He knew anything he said would sound awkward. So he simply kissed her hungrily and, as she tongued him back, lowered her to the leather sofa and mounted her like an old friend. As he entered her, she gasped in surprise but spoke only with her body, afraid to break the spell, as she wrapped her arms and legs around him to consume him all the way.

As they rutted quietly but passionately, he could tell she was as hard up as he was. Her husband had to be as crazy as she said. But she'd told the truth about being experienced, too. So they climaxed fast together.

As they came up for air, still coupled, Morgana sighed and said, "Oh, that was lovely, Darling. But it's only fair to warn you I really mean to go home and marry the boy next door—one of these days."

"Don't tell me everything," he growled. "Let me guess once in a while. You weren't planning on ditching me in the next few minutes, were you?"

She moved her hips teasingly, milking his semi-sated shaft with her trained internal muscles as she purred, "Hardly! My God, I'd almost forgotten how good this felt. Let me get on top if you're too tired to move that lovely thing in me some more!"

He wasn't too tired, but it sounded like fun so they changed places. As he lay on the smooth leather she playfully kissed his erection to full attention, then guided it in as she settled atop him with a sensuous sigh. She started moving up and down like a kid on a naughty merry-go-round as she observed, "Oh, it feels even deeper this way. But wait, I want to try something daring."

She slid her long smooth legs up over his chest and crossed them with his head between the outsides of her calves as she leaned back and braced her weight on her arms with her hands on his knees. The results were almost as alarming as they were pleasant. Morgana's trim buttocks were pressed together between his thighs and his shaft felt like it was being gripped in the jaws of a moist velvet vise. She started moving up and down again as she asked, "Doesn't that feel nice and tight?"

"Jesus," he said, "I think you're cutting off my circulation!" as he ran his hands up and down her inclined torso, noting that her bouncing breasts were almost out of reach. She knew what he wanted and straightened enough to let him fondle one in each hand as she teased them both with her new-found position. It was exciting, but it cramped his style as well as his shaft. He tried to help with thrusts of his own but finally said, "I don't think this is going to work. It could take all night to come in this position, Doll."

"I know," she said. "Isn't it marvelous? I *want* to make it last. I don't ever want it to end and we come so fast the other way."

He ran his right hand down her writhing torso and began to finger her clit with his thumb as he toyed with her pubic hair with his other fingers and said, "Let yourself go, Doll. This is cruelty to animals."

She shuddered with pleasure as her engorged clit responded to his skilled massage, but she pleaded, "Don't make me come so soon, Dick. I'm not ready to stop yet."

"Who said anything about stopping? I'm just getting my second wind."

"Really? Are you saying you can come more than twice in a row?"

"With you? You have to be kidding! What do you think I am, a sissy?"

She giggled, gave a great sigh, and rolled off, saying, "It's no use. I can't hold out another instant! Do it to me, Dick. Do it to me hard as you can!"

That was what he'd had in mind. But it was dark and they were both disoriented as he groped his way back into her and started pounding. She gasped, "Wait! Where on earth are we?"

"Who cares?" he answered, as he started moving faster. She wrapped her arms around his neck and gasped, "I'm falling!" but he didn't let her. He had her rump on the arm of the sofa, with his knees on the seat, and the angle was fantastic. Morgana liked it too, once she figured out where they were and that she couldn't really brain herself on the tile floor. Morgana let go of him and leaned back, saying, "Wheee!" as he pounded her even deeper with her buttocks braced on the padded arm rest while she did a back bend just brushing the floor with her long blond hair. She'd started the evening with her hair pinned Victorian, but now that she was getting used to his company, she'd let down her hair indeed.

He ejaculated in her, whipped it out, and rolled her over on the arm rest so that her lap was against the padding, her buttocks aimed up at him as he put it back in her to try for another at a novel angle. Morgana braced her palms on the floor and arched her spine, sobbing, "Oh, my God, I seem to have created a monster, and I love it!"

At that moment the door crashed open and some silly son-of-a-bitch was shining a flashlight in on them. Captain Gringo knew it wasn't Gaston, so he reached across Morgana's upthrust rump for the .38 on the end table and shot whoever it was. Morgana screamed, biting down on his erection with her vagina as the revolver roared, the light went out, and she came, all at once!

It felt swell. But Captain Gringo withdrew and ran over to the doorway, putting another round into a dimly visible figure flopping around like a seal on its belly on the rain-soaked patio bricks. He stopped flopping and just lay there. Across the way, Gaston called out, "Dick?" and the tall American yelled back, "One down, maybe more to go! Stay put. I can't see a fucking thing!"

A bullet spanged off the wet stucco near Captain Gringo as someone fired at the sound of his voice. He fired back at the muzzle flash and crabbed to one side before anyone could return the favor.

They didn't. The wind and rain whirling around the patio made it impossible to hear if his own shot had gotten any results. Then Gaston, bless him, hurled the oil lamp from Pepita's room to smash and explode in a pool of burning oil on the patio bricks. The wind tried to blow the orange flames out; the rain tried to douse them, but the oil spread hissing and spitting on the wet bricks, illuminating the four sides of the patio. Captain Gringo saw the first guy he'd nailed was wearing white cotton peon duds and had dropped a wicked machete as well as his bullseye flash. Another guy who looked like a peon, lay spread-eagled in an archway across the way. Captain Gringo moved around the arcade, feeling a little dumb. But nobody commented on his nudity and it sure beat wandering around in a hurricane fully clad. The light was still on in Morgana's room and the door still shut. He saw the second one he'd shot had dropped a cheap Spanish Star .32 between his bare feet. There was nobody else still hanging around.

He reached Pepita's door. Gaston was holding it ajar to ask what was up as the last flames hissed out, plunging them back into swirling ink. "False alarm," Captain Gringo said. "Couple of cat burglars trying to take advantage of the storm."

"One hopes you have a reason for such hopes, Dick?"

"Sure, more than one reason. In the first place, killers or kidnappers don't hit a house with one lousy whore pistol between them. They were a pair of ragged-ass pobrecitos, not hired guns. In the second place they passed up the bedroom Morgana should have been in and made for the parts of the house they hoped to find deserted at this hour. They were after the silverware, not us."

Gaston considered and replied, "Eh bien, it works. But what do we tell the constabulary about those gunshots when they arrive?"

"What constabulary? What gunshots? Listen to that *wind* upstairs! It's bad enough down here between the walls. Out on the street if anyone's dumb enough to be patrolling, they can't hear other sounds or judge directions enough to matter. Is Pepita awake in there?"

"*Merde alors,* what a stupid question. But get your own girl."

"Got one. We have to get those two stiffs under cover

between now and the cold gray, whether it's still blowing or not."

"Ah, I see the method in your madness. Leave it to me and the chica. There must surely be a discreet storeroom to slide them into. But they won't keep long, Dick. It's cold outside for the tropics, but not *that* cold."

"Hell, they won't really stink for a good twelve hours."

"That's what I just said. We're a long way from the ocean, too."

"I know. That's why they have to stay here. But *we* don't. After you stash the stiffs, try to get some beauty rest. We're pulling out at 0500 hours."

Gaston frowned and asked, "Are you mad? It will still be dark and the hurricane will still be raging, Dick!"

"I sure hope so. The more serious guys looking for Morgana won't be expecting us to make a break for it at such a foolish time. So, when you think about it, it's not that foolish a time."

Morgana thought he was crazy, too. But she'd enjoyed some of the mad positions he'd suggested before they caught a few winks in each other's arms and, what the hell, she didn't have a *better* plan. So, in the wee small hours she grumbled herself into the most sensible clothes and the stoutest pair of shoes she owned as Captain Gringo, already dressed, saw to a few last chores about the house before they cut out.

Gaston found him in the storeroom, busting up empty wooden boxes and piling the resultant kindling on the two dead burglars in the corner. Gaston said, "It won't work. No wood fire can reduce a body completely to ashes, Dick."

The American nodded and said, "I'm hoping they'll find enough bones to make it two people killed in an accidental fire, period. Morgana's crazy husband is looking for this house. When he finds it, I want them to tell him Morgana used to live here, but that she and her servant girl seem to have burned to death during the hurricane, see?"

"Ah, oui, that might work. The poor dears obviously sought shelter here as the storm winds frightened them and, obviously, one or the other was *très* careless with the lamp, non?"

"You'd make a great detective. Naturally, if anyone really examines the charred skeletons, they'll figure out they were a couple of guys. But who's going to? This storm will have left a few other stiffs for them to worry about."

"I said I had that part imbedded in my brain, Dick. But do you think it wise to set fire to a house as we are trying to make a discreet move to safer quarters? I have always noticed fires attract crowds, even in a wind storm."

"I'm counting on that, too. We'll use a candle as a time fuse and be a good quarter mile away when the coal oil and lumber goes poof. Anyone dumb enough to be out on the streets in this storm this early in the morning should come running this way while we run the other."

"Run *what* other, *sacre le goddamn?*"

"Over the river and into the woods, to Grandmother's house or Belize—whichever comes first. We can't leave Pepita behind to say they went thataway. Do you think you have her on our side?"

"*Oui*. She has been on my side since I got in her inside. But seriously, Dick, we can't follow the coast trail south in this *très fatigue* hurricane. It's under at least ten feet of water with floating timber and various types of reptilian life forms at the moment."

"Yeah. We'll have to hack our own path with that machete these burglars were kind enough to bring along. Get the gals and make sure they're set to make a break for it while I finish here."

Gaston left, muttering to himself while Captain Gringo piled more tinder on the bodies and found a can of lamp oil to pour over the mess. He was just about finished when Morgana burst in on him, saying, "Gaston said you're going to set my house on fire!" and he explained, "It's not your house. It's the landlord's house and I'll explain when we're on our way. Don't you have a slicker or poncho, Morgana?"

"No. This poplin travel duster is the stoutest garment I brought with me from the hacienda. Gaston says my umbrella doesn't sound practical."

"Gaston's right. Okay, we'll all dry out when and if the sun ever comes back out. Head for the gate and wait with Gaston and your chica. I think I know what I'm doing. But you could get your eyebrows singed if I'm wrong."

She didn't leave. He didn't have time to argue. He dribbled the last of the coal oil across the tile floor in a narrow line then put the lit candle gingerly in place, saying, "When this burns down to the floor it will either go out or there's going to be a hell of a poof. So let's haul ass!"

He grabbed Morgana's elbow and led her out and down the arcade to where Gaston, Pepita, and the machete were waiting. Gaston opened the gate without being told and the hurricane winds roared in at them so hard the rain drops felt like buck shot. Morgana flinched and gasped, "We can't go out in *that*!" But Captain Gringo didn't give her any choice. Pepita was pissing and moaning as Gaston dragged her out, too. Once they were on the street they couldn't tell if the girls were screaming or not—the hurricane winds blotted out all sounds. The visibility was nil and the narrow street between the solid walls on either side was shin deep in water running seaward. Captain Gringo didn't want to go to sea, so he took the lead and bulled through the howling darkness against the current. He knew if he kept going uphill long enough they had to hit the jungle west of town. He bumped into all sorts of other things in the dark, mostly wet stucco, and wound up carrying Morgana before they crashed into wind-whipped wet vegetation and noticed the water was only ankle deep and the wind wasn't howling quite so loud. He wedged Morgana in the lee of an ancient fig tree and called out, "Gaston, are you and Pepita still with us?"

Gaston croaked, "*Oui,* but I am très certain we both drowned a mile back! Where on earth are we, Dick? It should be getting light by now and hurricanes are supposed to blow themselves out sooner or later. But, *regardez,* it is still black as pitch and blowing harder than when we started!"

"Yeah," Captain Gringo said, "let's work our way deeper into the trees and see if it helps."

Morgana said something about her clothes he didn't hear clearly. Still carrying her, he bulled blindly into the Honduran Rain Forest, which was living up to its name beyond all common sense. Wet branches lashed his face, and from the noise she was making, Morgana was getting whipped pretty good, too. But it couldn't be helped. There was no sense trying to machete a path when one couldn't see to swing a machete. A branch snagged his hat. He let it go. The wind conditions were rapidly improving and the rain still hitting them through the tree canopy couldn't get them any wetter than they already were. He tripped over a root and fell, twisting to avoid landing atop Morgana with his full weight as they crashed together upon the soggy forest floor. He called out, "Watch it, Gaston. We're down and in enough trouble without you stepping on our faces!"

Gaston and Pepita joined them and simply plopped down beside them in the muck. Pepita was crying. Gaston said, "Oink, oink, isn't this fun? I always wondered what it would feel like to wallow like a pig in the mire. Do you have any idea where we are, Dick?"

"No," Captain Gringo answered, "but let's stay here for now. We sure as hell couldn't have left any footprints and we have to be under cover. What time is it, Gaston?"

"*Merde alors,* how should I know? It was about five when we left the house and I'm sure we've been floundering about out here for a week or so. Why?"

"Dawn comes fairly regular at six A.M. in the tropics. Do you suppose it's been cancelled this morning for some reason?"

"I *know* the reason, you floundering duck! But wait, I think I can see my hand before my eyes now!"

Captain Gringo raised his own hand experimentally, waved it, and said, "Things *are* looking brighter, at that. I can't see my hand before my face when I look directly at it. But I do see movement out of the corners of my eyes."

Morgana shuddered against him and said, "You should have let me drown myself the easy way. All at once. I'm freezing, Dick. Couldn't we have a campfire while we're waiting out this storm?"

He snorted in disgust, "Hell, you couldn't keep a *cigar* lit right now. We're still too close to town to light a campfire if we could. I don't want to expose our position."

She laughed bitterly, and said, "Some position. It feels like we're sprawled together across a soggy mattress under a cold shower! I'm soaked to the skin and chilled to the bone and I see no sign of a break in this perishing storm. Can't you think of any way to warm us up a bit, Dear?"

He started to unbutton her duster. She giggled, "Don't be silly. That's not what I meant."

He rolled half atop her and went on unbuttoning as he replied, "Let's be practical, Doll. It's not like we're strangers and it's a good way to warm at least *part* of us."

Her voice dropped to a whisper as he found the blouse and skirt under the duster were indeed soaking wet and clinging to her chilled curves. She protested, "What about the others?" and he said, "Relax. They're being practical, too, on the other side of a tree."

"Really? I don't hear anything but the wind and rain."

"Don't have to hear, to know what Gaston's doing. The only time he ever shuts up is when he has a mouth full. We may as well get out of all this soggy cloth. It's not doing us a bit of good and it's sure in the way."

But as he went on undressing her, Morgana said. "Wait, Dear. I know we did get rather carried away back at the house, earlier, but I've had time to come to my senses and . . ."

"I wish you dames wouldn't do that," he cut in, adding, "I used to think it was the cold gray light of dawn, but since it's still dark, it must be post-climactic depression, right?"

Her thighs were frog-belly cold and clammy as he wedged his hand between them to reassure her with some friendly petting. She tried to cross her legs as she said, "Dick, I'd be fibbing if I said I didn't like to fuck. But let's be serious. I'm really very fond of you, but I really mean to go home to England if we ever get out of this mess and . . ."

"Hey, who ever said we were more than pals, Morgana? I'm not trying to get you to fall in love with me. I'm just trying to warm you up."

"Oh, you certainly are," she sighed, as she opened her thighs to allow him a better grip on her groin. The thatch between her legs was as cold and wet as the pants he still had on. So, as he started to finger her he asked her to do something about his buttons, too. She started with his fly. But as she reached in to fondle his semi-erect and frozen love tool, she said, "You must think I'm a shameless wanton. I've always been taught you were only supposed to have sex with people you were in love with. But I do want this in me, and I want it *now*!"

They were still half-dressed, but they had most of the important parts exposed to the elements, so he rolled aboard her. It felt wild as hell. Her belly and thighs were ice cold against his skin. It made her insides feel warmer and yummier than ever. She giggled, "My God, it feels like you poked an icicle up me. But don't stop. It seems to be warming up and . . . oh, yes, *do* it, Dick!"

So he did. Between the discomfort of the cold rain on his back and the fact he'd had her already that night, it took him longer than usual to climax. She took that as a compliment. He grinned to himself in the darkness as he remembered what Gaston had once said about men and women both deserving something better as sexual partners. The gods had built both sexes too different to enjoy each other naturally. That was why married men cheated with whores and married women hired gigolo boys. To really enjoy recreational sex, one's partner had to remain detached enough to concentrate on screwing right. He wasn't totally disinterested as he skillfully laid Morgana in the rain. No normal man could have been. But he was having his own morning-after thoughts and, great as she was, she sure was getting to be a problem.

He wasn't sorry he'd helped her. Any human being deserved help unless they were trying to hurt you. But he'd never expected, when he talked her out of leaping in the harbor, to be stuck with her so long. He knew she was pretty confused about it, too. But what could they do about it? She needed help and a gentleman doesn't desert a lady in distress even when she *doesn't* put out.

Morgana wasn't as detached, now. She was bumping and grinding to meet his skilled if distracted thrusts and as she got hotter she started clawing off her clothes, sighing, "Oh, it does feel nicer, naked." So he propped himself up on stiff elbows to allow her to squirm the blouse and skirt off over her head, still lying on her open duster. As he settled back down on her he had to admit it was a hell of an improvement. So he faked an orgasm and called time out to peel his own wet things off. By the time he was down to nothing but his boots and shoulder holster, and they were going at it again, the rain seemed less uncomfortable. Her wet naked belly and breasts felt cozy-warm and the cold wind on his rollicking rump inspired it to sustained effort. But in truth, he was getting a bit sated in the same old rut and the next time he ejaculated he had to stop and just lay in her arms, recovering breath and inspiration. She moved teasingly and asked, "Can't we do it some more, Dick? I'm just starting to feel human again."

"You feel better than human. But I'm *only* human. Let's just let it soak a while and see what comes up. You sure were telling the truth about not having had any for a while, weren't you?"

She laughed roguishly and replied, "I told you we'd created a monster. I think my fear and hatred of that maniac I married must have made my mind forget how nice it could be. But my body must have been terribly frustrated all this time, judging from the way it's been acting ever since I met you. You know what I like most about you, Dick? It's the feeling of, well, *freedom* you inspire in me. I feel I can tell you anything, or suggest anything, without you trying to shame me. I almost wish I didn't have to go back to England so soon."

"Hey, let's not talk *dirty*! Of course you're going back, as soon as we can get you to the next port of call. But don't worry. It'll take us at least three or four days and nights on the trail to Belize. By that time we'll have tried every position and should be willing to part friends."

"You're awful," she laughed, "but I'm looking forward to it. I must be awful, too, because I know what you mean. Do you think it's wrong to, well, do this just for fun, without the complicated muck?"

"The complicated muck can be nice, too, with the right

person. I try not to fall in love, though. My life is complicated enough as it is. I've no right to drag a permanent lover along. Sometimes it's complicated enough making sure *Gaston* doesn't take a bullet meant for me."

She said she understood, kissed him, then added, "Speaking of Gaston . . . is that him or a white rabbit over there to our west?"

Captain Gringo followed her gaze and chuckled. The light was getting a little better now, albeit with no improvement in the weather. It was still too dark to make out details and the dusky Pepita was still invisible, but that sure did look like a pale white rump bouncing up and down maybe twenty yards away.

Morgana said, "They certainly seem to be going at it hot and heavy."

"Yeah, well, he's French. He doesn't often get anything as young as your chica. So he's probably showing off."

Morgana contracted her internal muscles on his shaft and pouted, "I wish *you'd* show off a bit, Dick." So he started moving again. It felt good. But he wished she hadn't put it that way. He'd reached that stage, all too familiar to reasonably virile and considerate men, where he could still keep it up but wasn't really hot enough to come. Morgana didn't seem to notice the difference as he started pounding her politely. The exercise was a good way to keep warm. But in truth, it was getting to feel more like a chore than lovemaking. He started counting, silently, to keep going with a promise to stop after a hundred strokes. He made them hard and fast, knowing he'd get a break sooner if he could make her come fast. It worked, or she said it did. He faked his own climax for sure as they went limp together. Neither said anything for a time. Then Morgana said, "My God, they're still at it."

Captain Gringo grinned; he knew why. He wondered what Gaston had counted to by now. Old Pepita seemed to take longer to get there. Wondering what Pepita felt like wrapped around a dong made his own twitch. Morgana said, "Oh, I felt that. Can we do it some more?"

He sighed, "No. Since we've agreed we're pals who can level with each other, I'm about out of steam."

"I'm not, and it's still raining cats and dogs. It feels so much warmer when we're screwing, Dick. *They're* still going at it. Why can't we?"

"I said he was French. Would you like to change partners for a while?"

"My God, what a dreadful thing to suggest!" she gasped, then giggled and added, "It sounds absolutely Roman. Have you ever done anything that wicked, Dick?"

"Honey, if I told you some of the wicked things I've done you'd probably faint. Swapping is just good clean fun. What the hell, we're not engaged and variety is the spice of life, right?"

She laughed and answered, "I confess part of the thrill when we started was the, well, newness of your sweet strange shaft. My God, what am I *saying*? Nice girls aren't supposed to even *think* like that!"

"Yeah, being a nice girl sounds boring as hell."

"You're right. I don't want to be nice right now. I'll have plenty of time to be nice when I get back to my proper little village. Let's be wicked some more."

He said okay and called out, "Hey, Gaston? You want to play musical laps?"

Morgana flinched and gasped, "Wait, that's not what I meant!" But he said, "Sure it is. You just can't admit you're as intrigued as I am."

Then, before she could argue further, he rolled off and rose naked in the rain and wind. Gaston approached in the same condition to ask, "What's up?" and Captain Gringo said, "Both of us, I hope. We're all going to be spending a lot of intimacies on the trail to Belize. So let's get down to basics."

Leaving Gaston and Morgana to sort things out as they

saw fit, Captain Gringo moved over to where Pepita lay under a quinine tree, as naked and wet. As he dropped beside her on her soggy poncho, the little mestiza gasped, *"Por favor, señor*! What is the meaning of this?" He didn't feel like having the same dumb argument. So he took Pepita in his arms and kissed her to shut her up. She kissed back great and as he ran his free hand over her dark strange body, he saw he'd made a great move. Pepita wasn't built any better than Morgana. She was simply built completely different. Her curves were rounder and softer, her lips fuller and her tongue inspired. He was inspired, too, as he rolled atop her, spread her shorter, chunkier thighs, and entered brand new territory. He hissed, "Oh, yeah!" as he sank to the roots in Pepita's hot tight jelly roll. She braced her heels against the wet cloth on either side of his thighs and started moving, not *better* but completely *different*. He didn't have to fake his passion, now. Nothing beat a completely strange crotch to inspire even a jaded male. As he started pounding Pepita, he cast a glance over his shoulder and, sure enough, the white blur of Gaston's naked rump was bouncing up and down over there like a happy bunny rabbit. Pepita moaned, "Oh, you are making me so happy, señor!" So he kissed her again, started moving even faster, and said, "I like to see *all* my pals happy, Querida!"

The storm didn't break, but an hour later it was light enough to see clearly in the jungle. As they all redressed, Morgana said she couldn't look any of them in the eye, ever again. Dames were like that.

Captain Gringo took the lead with the machete, bearing due south, if he was judging the wind right. There wasn't as much underbrush to clear as one might have expected. The thickest jungle tangles were always near pathways and streams. He figured they were at least a dozen miles from town when two nice things happened simultaneously: the wind died down and he hacked a path into a clearing. He could see slash and burn farmers had cleared a milpa and deserted it after a recent harvest. The burned-over soil was carpeted with shin-deep grass, but the weeds hadn't taken over yet. He stopped, turned to the others, and said, "Let's hole up here and see if the sun comes out. It looks as if we're in the eye of the hurricane."

Gaston started gathering wood without being asked to. A few minutes later the sun came out and Captain Gringo grinned at the two confused girls and said, "See? What did I tell you? Let's all strip and dry our duds out on the grass before we push on."

Morgana looked past him as she murmured, "You can't be serious. It's broad daylight!"

"Hey, you can't dry your clothes in the sun at *night*, Doll. Don't worry about it. There's nobody around for miles."

"You two *men* are, damn it!"

"So what? Are Gaston and I strangers? I thought we'd agreed to be practical, Morgana."

"Don't be beastly. Just because a girl gets, well, a bit carried away in the dark doesn't mean she's ready to join a nudist colony! About last night, Dick . . ."

"We all know what happened last night and later this morning and it was swell. I'm not suggesting a daylight orgy, Honey. We've got to dry our skin and clothes before we go on. Aside from catching cold you can pick up all sorts of fungus and stuff romping around in soggy jungles."

Gaston had been listening as he started the fire with some difficulty and a handful of dry punk he'd dug from a fallen timber. He stood up and started taking off his clothes, saying, "Perhaps if I broke the ice, non?"

Captain Gringo nodded and started taking his own clothes off. Pepita giggled and, since she was simply dressed in the first place, peeled off her wet garments to stand demurely brown and naked by the fire, asking, "Which one of you wants to make love to me now?"

Morgana stamped her foot and said, "Now cut that out! I know I acted silly, in the dark, but I'm really not that kind of a girl!"

"Be a wallflower, then," Gaston laughed. "Perhaps Pepita would like to play *la sandwich?*"

"Skip it, Gaston," Captain Gringo replied. "It's more important to get dry and put some more miles between ourselves and Corozal than it is to play grab-ass. We'll have plenty of time for fun and games between here and Belize."

But naturally it didn't work out that way. Morgana waited until her three companions had squatted nude and happy around the little fire before she laughed a bit wildly, took off her own wet clothes, and spread them beside theirs on the grass to dry. As she hunkered down between Captain Gringo and Gaston, she giggled again and warned, "Don't get ideas. The only reason I'm not squatting like a savage across the fire from you is that it would be even more embarrassing to have the two of you staring at my poor abused body. I say, what do we do about breakfast?"

Captain Gringo said, "We don't. It only hurts the first day. I'm going to try and avoid the small settlements between here and Belize. A two or three day fast never hurt anybody and we can find water almost anywhere in this semi swamp."

"Oh, God, I've been half drowned, screwed silly, and now he wants to put me on a *diet*! Seriously, Dick, do you think the natives would hurt us?"

"No, but they'd *remember* us. You and Pepita were supposed to have died in that fire back there. The whole plan's a wasted effort if a mess of coastal Indians and simple villagers see a white woman wandering through their jungle. Girls like you are a novelty away from the main colonial centers."

"Oh, well," she sighed, "I suppose I could stand to lose a few pounds. Don't *stare* at me, damn it."

He shrugged and said, "They say meat's more tender closer to the bone. Speaking of pounds, I still have my wallet. Where are you carrying your own money, Morgana?"

"In the pocket of my duster, of course. Why?"

"It's probably soaking wet. You'd better spread the notes out to dry in the sun. Then we'll wrap them better."

"All right. I'll fetch them. But please don't stare at me. I'm trying to be a good sport and I know it's silly, but I'm just not used to being naked in front of God and everybody."

He nodded and stared at the fire as she rose. Out of the corner of his eye he saw Gaston had Pepita on her back and was fooling around with her again. He felt a little embarrassed, too. But what the hell could he say?

Morgana came back, dropped to her naked knees beside him, and sobbed, "Dick, the money's gone! It must have fallen out back there when we were being silly! We have to go back for it!"

He grimaced and said, "No way. Even if we could find the place, it's the wrong direction. Your husband has to be as nuts as you say if he's been letting a dish like you sleep alone, and nuts make me nervous."

"But, Dick, it was all the money I had in the world! How am I to get home to England, now?"

"First we have to get you to Belize. Don't worry. We'll work something out. Gaston and I still have a few bucks. And what the hell, holding up a bank sounds safer than tangling with El Cazador and his hunting companions."

She wiped a tear from her eye as she said, "I don't understand why you're going to so much trouble for me. Surely it's more than sex?"

"Hey, don't knock the icing on the cake, Honey. Don't worry about why we're helping you, either. We're *always* in trouble, so what the hell. It seems to make more sense when you can tell yourself you're saving a maiden in distress instead of just running for your miserable lives."

"I could hardly call myself a maiden, now," she chuckled. "Oh, my God, look at those two!"

Gaston and Pepita were going at it dog-style. It did look sort of silly. But it was giving him a hard-on. So he looked away and said, "Let's talk about something else, unless you'd like to *try* it."

Back in Corozal, in the lobby of the best hotel in town, a furtive figure in wilted linen was reporting to a sleekly good-looking man wearing a mushroom whipcord safari outfit. The tracker said, "I have grim news, El Cazador! The house your woman rented has burned to an empty shell. The charred remains of two were found in the ruins. The English fire fighters think La Señora and her chica must have been trapped by the flames."

El Cazador shrugged and replied, "So? Then Morgana has paid for disobeying her lord and master. I regret she got off so easily. But enough about the English cow. What else have you to tell me about the fools who stepped in as she was about to kill herself as I planned?"

"We are still working on their names, El Cazador," the tracker answered. "Informants along the waterfront told the men you had watching her that they are soldiers of fortune, known to have visited these parts before. But, forgive me, I mean no disrespect, but I fail to see why we are hunting *them*. Apparently they simply escorted your late wife home and left, since they were not found dead in the ruins. What did they do to offend you so, El Cazador?"

El Cazador smiled dreamily and said, "For one thing they interfered in my affairs. For another, I like to hunt. It's more sporting to hunt when one has a reason, however slight, for tracking the quarry, no?"

The tracker nodded. He didn't agree, since he wasn't as crazy as his employer. But El Cazador paid well for faithful service, and killed when one disagreed with him.

This time he hoped he wouldn't have to watch when the boss caught up with them. The tracker was a cold-blooded killer of man and beast, but he only killed for profit. El Cazador tended to finish off his victims in a way that made even a professional butcher want to puke.

Fortunately for their temporary peace of mind, Captain Gringo and his companions weren't certain whether El Cazador was still after them as they frolicked in the grass a few miles away.

Getting Morgana to go for public sex had taken a little argument, but once she lay back and let Captain Gringo mount her, with assurances the other couple were too busy to peek, she seemed to warm to the occasion and, like most young ladies raised Victorian, had more interest in the subject and a wilder imagination than Her Majesty was said to approve of. The smaller, darker, plumper Pepita hadn't been raised with any rules inhibiting her natural appetites, and seemed inclined to show off. So once Morgana was warmed up enough to forget her initial shyness she had to uphold the natural superiority of the Anglo-Saxon by topping Pepita in what could best be described as a very bawdy game of follow the leader. By the time their clothes were dry they were all on very friendly terms indeed.

Captain Gringo felt a drop of rain on his back as he was holding Pepita's head in his lap and called out,

"Party's over, boys and girls! We'll be drier under the trees when the second wall of the hurricane hits. Ball your duds in tight bundles and carry them tucked under your arms. That way, if it ever stops raining we'll have reasonably dry stuff to put on."

They did as he suggested, but Morgana said she felt silly strolling through the jungle naked as a babe. Captain Gringo didn't answer. He was getting tired of telling her she was only doing what came naturally. It seemed sort of silly for her to go coy again after they'd just played daisy chain. He couldn't think of a part of her, or Pepita, he hadn't had a pretty good look at by now. But apparently when a proper English girl wasn't trying to service two men and another girl at the same time, she wanted them to think of her as bashful.

The wind and rain hit them from the opposite quarter and they got to cool off as they trudged head down through the storm and the jungle. It was still blowing like hell when it got too dark to see again. But the rain was letting up. This time the main thrust of the hurricane seemed to have been ahead of the eye. So when he called a halt for the night, Captain Gringo told everyone to put their clothes on. It helped. He still wasn't ready to risk a night fire. But they huddled together reasonably warm and dry in the lee of a big fallen mahogany. The advantage of the earlier orgies lay in the fact they now were all relaxed enough with one another's bodies to huddle close as they dozed. They were all too worn out to even think about sex.

They were awakened at dawn by the howling of birds and the song of an amazingly musical monkey. The wind and rain had stopped. It was not only light enough to travel but promising to be a hot day for hiking. So Captain Gringo took the lead, the others behind him bitching about not having breakfast.

It got worse. A crow could have made it to Belize flying fifty miles in a beeline. They had to walk around all sorts of stuff. It was a lot cooler in the jungle shade than it would have been otherwise, but the trees cut them off from the trade winds that made this part of the world habitable and Captain Gringo set a pace that made them sweat in the high humidity of the soggy rain forest. Later, the girls would remember the trek as taking at least a week. It was only two days and nights, but Captain Gringo and Gaston would remember it with mixed feelings, too. They didn't meet any wild beasts more ferocious than mosquitos, but the mosquitos of the mosquito coast were enough to worry about. Captain Gringo's inland course through uninhabited jungle kept them away from both honest and dishonest natives. But the walking sure was tedious. It takes roughly a thousand paces to cover a mile—on a paved road. Try it over fallen logs, around ponds of sluggish alligators, then plaster each sole with heavy wet jungle muck and you'll lose interest in counting before you've covered many miles.

But it could have been worse. Their empty bellies stopped growling after the first twenty-four hours and at least there was no lack of water. One could reach up and grab a handful of leaves to suck like a sponge without even slowing down. (Naturally, nobody but an idiot would have risked the standing water they waded through or around.) The two girls were good sports about fasting as well as fornicating. So there was only a little bitching on the long hot trail and lots of billing and cooing at night.

Captain Gringo navigated by his watch and the way the streams they forded ran. Gaston kept saying they were hopelessly lost. But, sure enough, one evening, just as Captain Gringo was wondering if they'd bypassed Belize, they cut a substantial roadway with wagon ruts in its red clay. He called a halt and said, "This wagon trace has to go somewhere important, and the seaport at Belize is the only important thing they've got around here. We'll make camp back in the brush a ways and follow it seaward when it's light again. Gaston, bed the girls down out of sight while I stand look-out here. I want to see if I can spot you from the road, here."

He couldn't. He heard Gaston and the girls laughing about something and made a mental note to tell them all to keep it down that night. But nobody coming down the road, mounted or otherwise, was likely to suspect a nearby camp. Anybody on the wagon trace this late would be moving fast.

He sat on a fallen log, reaching for a smoke, then remembered he'd smoked his last claro that morning. So he settled for a twig to chew. Gaston came back to join him. The Frenchman straddled the log and said, "Dick, we have a problem. With nothing else to occupy her limited imagination, Pepita has become *très* enthusiastic about oral sex."

Captain Gringo chuckled fondly and said, "I noticed. When did *Frenchmen* start complaining about *that*?"

"*Eh bien,* I agree she gives delightful flute concerts, but now she has started teaching the English girl the delights of Sappho, and Morgana seems a willing pupil indeed!"

Captain Gringo shrugged and said, "She probably enjoys the variety. God knows we've all tried everything *else* together by now. I still don't see the problem, Gaston. *I* sure as hell don't want to go down on any lady who hasn't had a bath in recent memory. When did you start feeling so puritanical about enthusiastic naked ladies?"

"*Merde alors,* I'm not concerned about bisexual experimentation. You always encounter that among women willing to indulge in group sex. They do not have our male inhibitions, since women are allowed to be sissies. The problem is that Morgana has promised the servant girl she will take her back to England with her."

"So what? Morgana can probably use a housemaid she has broken in right. She tells me things are sort of dull in the village she came from."

"*Oui,* I know the advantages of having a well-trained staff when a lady has a reputation as well as her own hot nature to worry about. *Our* problem is that Morgana seems to think you promised to book her passage home."

"I did. I know it's dumb, but what the hell else can we do with her when we reach Belize?"

"Shoot her? Seriously, Dick. We don't have the wherewithall to spare for even *one* steamer ticket to Southampton. Sending them *both* will break us!"

Captain Gringo thought and said, "When you're right you're right. But we've still got to do it, unless you can think of something better. We can't just leave the poor dames stranded in a strange town and I can't see dragging them all the way to Limon with us, can you?"

"*Mais non,* it's been great fun, but alas the dew is off the rose and right now I'd trade them both for a warm meal. But let us consider this stranding business. I agree it seems a bit cold, but is it not *practique* as well? After all, what do we owe either of the little tramps?"

Captain Gringo frowned and said, "Hey, don't talk dumb. Neither one of them invited. We asked. How come a guy who likes to screw is a sportsman and a gal who lets him screw her is a tramp?"

Gaston sighed and said, "Spoken like a Frenchman. You were less trouble when you still thought West Point, my willing pupil. *Eh bein,* let us admit my remarks about their morals were unjust. That still leaves us with the financial problem. And even if we call them jolly comrades, I still fail to grasp why we have to go broke for them. We saved Morgana from her rather grotesque husband, damn it. Pepita's in no danger from anyone or anything but her own nymphomania. When do we, as you Yankees say, get off the hook?"

"When we see the ladies safely home, Gaston. Those are the rules where I come from. When you invite a lady out, no matter how things turn out, you owe it to her to see her safely home before you kiss her bye-bye, see?"

"It sounds absolutely Presbyterian. What if she's a fatiguing date?"

"You still see her safely home. Only a shit deserts a lady in midstream once he's agreed to escort her anywhere. Sometimes it can be a pain in the ass. But a gent plays the game by the rules."

He chuckled as he remembered a weekend leave from West Point and added, "Sometimes it can be the best revenge, since we're not allowed to beat a dreary dame up. I remember this impossible little bitch I was stuck with one night. I was really tempted to just ditch her in a dozen nasty places before I managed to get her home. She must have been used to men leaving her to pick up the tab and find her own cab. I pulled a switch that rattled her pretty good. But never mind all that. Neither Morgana nor Pepita have been anything but very nice to both of us, so . . ."

"*Merde alors,* I see you mean to see *those* two safely home no matter what I say. Tell me the end of the story about the bitch in New York. What did you do for your revenge, rape her in her vestibule?"

Captain Gringo laughed, "That would have been crude. Besides, I really didn't like her, so why should I have done her such a favor?"

"But you said you had a grand revenge."

"I did, according to her girlfriend, who was dating another cadet. You see, I just put up with her evil disposition and cock-teasing without batting an eye. I showed her the best time I could imagine, considering her mouth, then I took her home, thanked her for a lovely evening, and left."

Gaston frowned and added, "I am missing something. You call that *revenge*?"

"I didn't care if I was getting revenge or not. I was only acting like a gentleman. But apparently that was what kicked her little brain in the balls, to hear her friends tell it. You see, she was so confused by being treated like the nice gal she wasn't that she wound up thinking, and bragging, that I was nuts about her."

"Ahah! One observes the light at the end of the tunnel. The only thing that hurts a bitch worse than a punch in the nose is the suspicion, and guilt, that she may have been a *foolish* bitch, hein?"

Instead of commenting further on his school days, Captain Gringo hissed, "Take cover!" And, since Gaston had heard the wagon wheels, too, he was already moving at the time.

So both soldiers of fortune were crouched in the trail-side brush, guns drawn, when the mule drawn dray of green bananas passed. The teamster and his helper weren't armed and neither seemed interested in the jungle on either side as they made for town with their produce. When they'd passed out of earshot, Captain Gringo said, "Good. We're closer to Belize than I thought, and there hasn't been any recent bandit stuff, if the peones don't worry about travelling unarmed with night falling. Let's go back and get some rest with the girls and we'll wander into town in the morning when we won't attract as much attention."

Gaston agreed and led him back to where he'd left the girls. It was still light enough to have a good view of what they were up to and the two men felt a little left out. Captain Gringo had never been tempted by homosexuality and Gaston's one or two experiments in the old Legion had left him convinced he just didn't like it. But Morgana and Pepita had apparently gotten tired of waiting and had started the evening orgy without them. They were both stripped and going sixty-nine on Morgana's spread travel duster, with Morgana on top. Neither said anything as the two men flopped down beside them. The girls had their mouths full.

Gaston muttered, "How droll. But it's just as well. At my age I have to watch my health, and since no duty calls, I shall see if I can dream about eating something more filling."

Suiting actions to his words, Gaston lay back with his head on a mound of reasonably dry leaves, placed his hat over his face, and proceeded to go to sleep. Captain Gringo thought it was a sensible idea. But he'd lost his hat. The girls didn't seem to give a damn no matter what he did. He watched, bemused, and told himself he'd rather have a warm bath and a warm meal right now. But it wasn't easy to stay disinterested with two naked ladies moaning with delight almost close enough to reach out and touch. He had Morgana's pale wriggling rump aimed at him, offering an astoundingly gynecological view of her end of the proceedings. The part in Pepita's black hair extended up into the pinker parting of Morgana's white buttocks. The peon girl's pink tongue was fluttering like a naughty butterfly sipping forbidden nectar from the open blossom of the white girl's femininity as Morgana's pretty little asshole winked at him. For some reason the view seemed to be giving him an erection.

On the other hand, he was tired, weak-kneed from hunger, and they hadn't invited him to join them. So he tried to ignore them for a while. But he didn't have anything to smoke or read and it wasn't as if there was anything *better* to do.

He wasn't ready to fall asleep just yet. So he started taking off his clothes. By the time he'd stripped, his erection had risen fully to the occasion and the girls were fingering as well as licking one another. He crawled over and knelt behind Morgana's upthrust derrier. He gently removed Pepita's fingers from her twat as he said, "You need a man for a man-sized job, kids," and suited action to his words by mounting Morgana from behind. Pepita laughed to see a pair of balls above her nose and Morgana gasped, "Oh! Is that you, Dick?" as she arched her spine to take it deeper. He asked her if it mattered who it was and she purred she didn't care who or what was in there right now, as long as he didn't take it out. So he didn't, and as Morgana went on eating Pepita, the little chica, not wanting to be left out, began to lick them both as he thrust in and out of Morgana. The white girl moaned, "Oh, Jesus, that feels marvelous" and he asked, conversationally, "Is that why you want to take Pepita back to England with you?"

Morgana didn't answer. She was growling like a puma as she ran her own tongue deep inside her "faithful servant" so he knew he'd asked a dumb question.

In the morning they waited until some farm folk were moving down the wagon trace to town and fell in behind them, too far back for the peons to notice and question them, but close enough to look like stragglers from the same party as they trudged into Belize.

Belize was a bigger seaport than Corozal, and though they must have presented a wilder than common appearance by now, nobody saw fit to yell for the cops as they made their way to a posada Gaston knew about. They left the girls to bathe and make themselves more presentable at the inn while they scouted the waterfront. Disheveled white women drew attention anywhere, but a couple of unshaven knockaround bums looked part of any waterfront scene, and in a British colonial port, Captain Gringo didn't stand out as much as usual.

There was a three-island freighter anchored out in the roads and Gaston said he not only knew her, but knew where the English purser drank when they were in port. Captain Gringo knew his unfortunately good likeness was staring down from the reward posters on many a purser's bulkhead. So he told Gaston to see about passage for the girls alone. They agreed to meet later at a sidewalk cafe Gaston knew down at the end of the quay.

Before they split up, he gave Gaston his share of the passage money and told him to take care of the details if he could swing a deal. It wasn't just that he hated goodbyes. He didn't want to attract attention to himself. Even in a British port, the mostly dusky native types tended to notice a tall blond anglo more than a short dark Frenchman and it was asking for trouble to be seen with a beautiful Anglo dame, as well.

He expected a long dull wait at the cafe, nursing drinks with the little he had left. It didn't turn out that way. As he walked along the quay he spotted a luxurious private yacht moored alongside. The name on the transome was new to him, but he knew his old pal Greystoke of British Intelligence got a buy on sign painters. So he just strode up the gang plank and when a crewman wearing a Hindu turban asked him where the hell he thought he was going, said, "Get out of my way or I'll kill you. Your boss owes me money. Tell him Captain Gringo's aboard and that I'll wait for him in the salon, where he keeps the booze!"

The East Indian considered fighting about it, decided it might not be a good idea, and padded forward to get Greystoke while Captain Gringo moved aft to the salon he knew so well. He went to the untended bar and helped himself to a fist full of dollar cigars from the humidor before he started building himself a tall Glen Spey and soda. He'd just settled down on the sofa with a drink in one hand and a smoke in the other when the sardonic sissy-looking Englishman who ran the so-called yacht for Whitehall came in, looking innocent as usual. He nodded at the drink in Captain Gringo's hand and said, "Jolly good idea. I think I'll have one, too."

Captain Gringo waited until Greystoke was building his

own drink before he said, "You fucked us, Greystoke."

Greystoke never batted an eye. He was too deadly a man to show any emotion unless someone was actually aiming a cannon at him. He came over to join the unshaven American and sat down, asking, "How did I manage that, Dick? I didn't think you went in for buggery."

"You sent us on a mission. We went. When we got back to Corozal you and this tub weren't there. Neither was the money you promised us on completion of the contract."

"Good Lord, you chaps were gone for over a month longer than anyone planned. I'm a busy man, Walker. How the devil was I supposed to know you were still alive?"

"Well we are, and we still haven't been paid. So take your cock out of my ass and put the money in my pocket and we'll be pals again."

Greystoke sipped his own highball as he searched for the right words. Captain Gringo knew he was going to say something awful before he murmured, "I'm afraid, ah, we have a problem, Dick. Whitehall cables that he's not too well pleased with the way your mission turned out."

"No shit? How come London knows so much about the mission if you had us down as killed in action?"

"Well, confidentially, we do have other people working for us in these parts, despite your tedious Yankee *Monroe Doctrine*. I really did lose track of you and Gaston, after you shot up that chocolate factory with a machinegun. But we managed to follow your rather terrifying career that far, and I must say you didn't carry out the orders you were given, Dick."

"What carry? What orders? You used Gaston and me as dupes, as usual. You hired us to deliver a couple of British agents up in the headwaters of the Hondo. You didn't tell us the whole plan. But I guess you're allowed to keep a few secrets from the hired help. The point is that we took your agents where you told us and that's all we were being paid to do. So when do we get our fucking money?"

"You don't," Greystoke said, flatly. Then, noting the look in Captain Gringo's eyes he quickly added, "Before you start breaking up the furniture, it wasn't *my* idea, Dick! I treid to get Whitehall to see it your way. But they were dreadfully upset when they learned you'd lost a steam launch, all that military hardware, and both our spies along the way. They seem to feel that if anyone owes any money, you and Gaston owe Her Majesty quite a sum right now."

"Screw Her Majesty. We did our part of the job with a mess of guys you should have warned us about shooting at us all the way! Gaston and me didn't kill your incompetent agents. The one that was supposed to be the innocent wife murdered the one that was supposed to be her husband. Then she got herself killed refusing to obey my orders in a fire fight. So you can't even say I failed to protect them. The mission was fucked up from the start. Gaston and me carried out our end of it. I want my money."

"Uh, I can let you have a few pounds from my pocket, Dick."

Captain Gringo started to tell the English spy master what he could do with the pocket money. Then he thought how hard it would be to spend if it were up Greystoke's ass and growled, "I'll take it. But you still owe me."

Greystoke looked relieved and reached in his jacket for his billfold as he said, "I know you've been treated rather shabbily, Dear Boy. If there's anything else I can do to make it up to you . . . ?"

"What have you got in mind? I only like to sleep with women."

"I know you don't believe me, but so do I. I mean if there were some, well, less expensive favor."

Captain Gringo shrugged and asked, "Can you get me a pardon?"

"No, unfortunately. But I can promise you won't be arrested here in British Honduras, until I have to leave, at any rate."

"That's no favor. That's called covering your own ass. But, okay, I have an English girl on my hands who needs to get back to Essex alive and stay that way when she gets there. Can do?"

"Perhaps. Tell me about her."

So Captain Gringo brought Greystoke up to date, leaving out the dirty parts. When he'd finished, Greystoke whistled softly and said, "I've heard of El Cazador. Your English girl is right. He's an utterly mad, dedicated bastard! Unfortunately, I can't have him arrested. He's under the protection of Mexico, even though he's a Spanish citizen, and El Presidente Diaz is a mad dedicated bastard, too!"

Captain Gringo nodded grimly and said, "I noticed that, the last time I was in Mexico. The girl told me El Cazador was a Latin American."

"She was wrong, even if she was mad enough to marry him. Actually he's not even Latin. Montalban's a Basque from the Spanish Pyrenees. All Basques are a bit odd, but Roderico Montalban makes even his rather aristocratic family dreadfully nervous. They sent him over here to protect the family name from scandal. As a youth, he had a distressing habit of shooting local peasants for sport and there are limits to that sort of thing, even in Spain."

"Morgana tells me he got kicked out of British Africa for gunning blacks for no particular reason."

"She did get to know him rather well, didn't she? But since he thinks her dead, I can tidy things up for her with a few cables. You say she'll be leaving here aboard that freighter, *Glencannon?*"

"Yeah, if Gaston can get her aboard."

"Not to worry. I know the purser has a drinking problem and always needs extra money. I'll cable Southampton and have some chaps waiting for her there. They'll have new identity papers for her and they'll see she gets home safely with nobody following her. You can forget her and her uffish husband."

Captain Gringo sighed and took another sip of booze. He didn't even want to think about El Cazador, but forgetting Morgana Harlow, whoever she was, was going to hurt the next time he found himself in a strange town with a hard-on. Come to think of it, Pepita hadn't been bad, either. He asked Greystoke about the servant girl and was assured an old school chum with British Immigration could turn her into a dusky Essex lass. So that was that.

He took the twenty pounds Greystoke offered and put them away. They added up to about a hundred in real money and they said a white man could live like a king down here for months on a hundred dollars. They were always saying dumb things like that about the tropics.

Greystoke said, "Before you go, it's odd you should mention a maniac up on the Mexican border. I do have a mission in mind for Yucatan, just north of Quintana Roo. It has nothing to do with El Cazador. Are you at all interested?"

Captain Gringo put his empty glass down, shook his head wearily at the Englishman, and said, "Greystoke, you have to be even crazier than you look! You just fucked me on one deal and now you offer me a chance to go into country where both the legal government and a maniac husband are thirsting for my ass!"

"Forget about both the Diaz government and El Cazador. I have a good cover for you and you'd be going into nearly deserted country where neither of them would ever expect to see a white man, let alone you. I know you feel cheated about the last deal, but I could make it up to you by asking Whitehall to agree to extra hazard pay and . . ."

"Like I said, crazy as a bedbug!" the American cut in, adding, "I don't want hazard pay. Hazards make me nervous. *You* make me nervous, too. So as long as you just met me half way I'm calling our relationship a friendly parting, and parting *poco tiempo,* you silly son-of-a-bitch!"

As he rose, Greystoke asked, wistfully, "Don't you even want to know what the deal is, Dick?"

Captain Gringo shook his head and headed for the hatchway, saying, "No. Every time I listen to you, somebody gets killed and sooner or later it's got to be *me*! So, like we say in Spanish, Adios, mother-fucker!"

By siesta time it cas hot as hell, even on the waterfront with the trade winds blowing steadily. That was why it was siesta time in all the sensible parts of Latin America. But Belize was a British colonial port and while the Brits seemed to want all the tropics, they'd never grasped the details of living in them. So the sidewalk cafe stayed open.

It was just as well. Gaston hadn't showed yet. Captain Gringo nursed a bottle of Stout and smoked another of Greystoke's cigars as he stared out across the heat-shimmered pavement and the tepid waters of the harbor. A few longshoremen were still working in the heat, poor bastards, but the quay was almost deserted at this hour. Nobody who didn't have to was about to go out in the noonday sun unless he was an Englishman, and even some of them were learning.

A short wiry man in tropic whites came around the

corner and sat down uninvited across the metal table from Captain Gringo. To really grasp the insult one had to have been born Hispanic, but Captain Gringo had knocked around enough down here to know that no polite Hispanic ever sat down, even with a friend he knew, without asking, "Permiso?"

But, what the hell, it was too hot for a fight and he figured the little fart could see he'd lose if he started one. So the American just stared soberly at the stranger and waited for him to make the next move. His move was to put a familiar planter's hat on the table between them and say, "You dropped this, Captain Gringo."

It was the hat he'd lost in the jungle, after leading Gaston and the girls away from the house in Corozal. He shrugged and said, "I used to have a hat like that. Where did you find it?"

The stranger smiled smugly and said, "Where you left it, of course. I have something else for you. But before we go any further, I must warn you certain friends of mine are covering us, should you go for the gun under that jacket."

Captain Gringo swallowed the sudden dryness in his mouth without letting it show as he nodded and said, "I finish fights. I hardly ever start them. What the hell is going on here?"

The stranger placed a roll of English pound notes wrapped with a rubber band next to Captain Gringo's hat. The American had seen the roll before. Morgana had showed him her money before they'd left her house. It was the money she'd lost in the jungle. He picked it up, tucked it away, and said, "You track pretty good."

"Thank you. It is my profession."

"I had that part figured out. Let me guess the rest. You and your pals work for El Cazador, right?"

"Ah, the poor unfortunate English woman told you about him before she perished back in Corozal, then?

Bueno, it saves needless discussion. I am called *El Tigre.* I am one of El Cazador's best trackers."

"No argument about that. Tell me, did you track us here the old-fashioned way or did you just figure out where we were going and head us off?"

"A little of both, Captain Gringo. We knew you and your friend had been seen with El Cazador's woman before the fire at her house. We knew you were not in the house with her and her servant girl when it burned. Ergo you had to be somewhere else, so we searched about until we cut your trail. In all modesty, it was not difficult. Few men your shoe size seem to have headed into the jungle in the middle of a hurricane. We trailed you to your first camp, found that money, then trailed you farther until it was obvious where you were going. Then, as you say, we headed you off. You may have noticed it takes much longer to get here by hacking through the jungle, no?"

Captain Gringo kept his voice light as he said, "Like I said, you're good. But tell me something. How come you didn't hit us in the jungle where you had us all to yourselves? No offense, but you're going to have a tougher time taking me here and now, even if you do have a back-up team across the way. I don't want to make you nervous, but if I go down, you, at least, are going with me."

El Tigre looked reproachful and answered, "Take you, señor? Is that any way to speak to a man who just gave you back your belongings? I, El Tigre, do not *take* the game I track. I am only paid to *find* it, for El Cazador."

Captain Gringo grimaced and said, "I gotcha. What's the point of this cat and mouse shit, Tigre?"

"Cat and mouse, señor? I play no cat and mouse with you. I bring you your belongings and you insult me with strange Yanqui notions. What is this game of cat and mouse you speak of, Captain Gringo? I am not familiar with the term."

"Bullshit. I've been down here long enough to suspect you folks invented it. But let me see, now, don't you Latin types call cat and mouse, *Tu Madre*?"

El Tigre laughed, boyishly, and said, "Oh, yes, that *is* a familiar old Spanish game. How do you like it, so far?"

"It's kind of boring. Okay, I got your message. El Cazador wanted me to know he was hunting me. So now I know. What am I supposed to do now, start running?"

"That is for you to say, señor. My employer, as you may have heard, has unusual views on sportsmanship. He has not arrived in town, yet. So you have the rest of the day to make any plans you wish. El Cazador is looking forward to the results. Since he knows *you* by reputation, too!"

"Wait a minute. Are you saying this jerk-off you work for is giving me a sporting stalk just because he thinks I make interesting quarry? I thought he was pissed-off because I kept his wife from drowning herself."

El Tigre shrugged and said, "Perhaps that gives him the excuse even a Basque needs, Captain Gringo. But you put it nicely when you say he simply enjoys hunting dangerous animals."

Before Captain Gringo could think of a way to answer that, Gaston came down the quay, frowned thoughtfully at El Tigre and sat down. Captain Gringo introduced them and told Gaston what the deal was. Gaston shrugged and said, "It sounds *très* juvenile. I took care of our more pressing problems here in town, Dick. So there is nothing to keep us here, except poverty."

Captain Gringo called for the waiter before he said, "We have enough money, now. Our pal, here, just returned the money we, uh, lost in the jungle."

El Tigre chuckled indulgently as Captain Gringo ordered drinks all around. Then he smiled thinly at Gaston and said, "You two do not wish for it to be known you were travelling with two native girls. It is most gallant. But do not worry. El Cazador prefers to hunt men. Your putas are safe, wherever you abandoned them."

Captain Gringo waited until the waiter brought the drinks before he laughed lightly, "You must have done some sniffing at our trail indeed. I don't remember using a rubber with those Indian gals, do you, Gaston?"

Gaston didn't answer as he stared at El Tigre over the rim of his stein. The tracker said, "One does not have to sniff deeply to read the signs of an orgy in damp soil. You must have had a good time with the putas you picked up. It was very amusing. One of my associates even thought, at first, the one in the high heels might have been a white woman. But I, El Tigre, read impressions in the soil like others read a book, and no stuffy Englishwoman ever served two men and another woman as wildly as that."

Captain Gringo said, "Go write dirty words on a fence. Then go tell your boss we accept the challenge, and that if he knows what's good for him he'll tuck his tail between his legs and scoot for home."

El Tigre nodded, drained his glass, and started to rise. But Gaston put one fatherly arm around his shoulders and said, "*Madames et M'siers,* let us not have an angry scene, here. We are all such good friends, non?"

El Tigre sat back down with an odd expression on his face as Gaston sort of braced him, like an old drinking buddy fixing to sing an Irish song or something. Gaston asked Captain Gringo, "Are we paid up here?"

"Sure, the drinks come to the table C.O.D. but what . . . Gaston, did you just do what I think you did to that guy?"

"*Oui.* Let us be on our way. The waiter should not come out in this heat unless someone calls for him, and even then it should take a while to notice he's not just drunk, hein?"

Captain Gringo got to his feet, sweeping the scenery

all around with his eyes as Gaston lowered El Tigre's head gently to the table top to let him "sleep it off." As Gaston slipped the knife back under his jacket, Captain Gringo growled, "Okay, he must have been bluffing. But that sure was a dumb risk to take, Gaston!"

"On the contrary, it was no risk at all. I naturally scouted all about the area before I approached a man I knew seated with one I did not. So I knew his tale of being covered was a bluff, long before I stabbed him. But let us discuss it along the way, hein? I don't think we should be here when El Cazador gets *our* message!"

Captain Gringo had to admit Gaston's reply to El Cazador had been more pointed than the one he'd meant to send back with El Tigre. It even made Captain Gringo nervous. His in with British Intelligence didn't give him a license to murder people in broad daylight on the streets of Belize, or to hang around with pals who did. British Honduras was policed by spiffy, well-trained West Indian constables, led by white officers trained by Scotland Yard in investigative work. He didn't want to talk to them about the guy they'd left sitting dead at the cafe table. He knew the constabulary would want to talk to *somebody* about it, and that they'd make the standard moves good cops were trained to. So the first thing they did was to go back to the posada to clean up and shave. Then they told the people there they were heading down the coast, went to a men's shop, and outfitted themselves with decent duds.

Looking twice as civilized as anyone along the waterfront would remember, they went to a decent hotel reserved for properly dressed whites, and checked in to third story rooms facing one another across the hallway. They had more than one reason for this, even though it made a hell of a dent in their new reserves.

Hotel clerks always suspected and remembered two guys sharing one room. It was very risky to pick locks on a guy with his buddy across the hall reading over your shoulder, and as Gaston observed, they could get lucky, and he wanted a little privacy with the *next* lady he ran into.

Captain Gringo agreed the romp through the jungle with Morgana and Pepita had been more raunchy than romantic, too. But as he checked his window shutters out he noticed the *S.S. Glencannon* was steaming out of the harbor, and he couldn't help missing the girls a little. He and Gaston had enough left between them to hole up respectable—maybe a week or more—if they went easy on the room service, booze, and broads. It cost ten times as much to live like proper gentlemen in the tropics than it did to just bum around. But he knew the constabulary would be looking for some waterfront bums in connection with Gaston's enthusiastic reply to El Cazador. So they had to look and act like guys who didn't hang around such neighborhoods.

The constabulary and El Cazador would doubtless be watching for anyone trying to leave town in a hurry, either by land or sea. So holing up in a good hotel in the middle of town should throw off the maniac hunting them, too. Unless, of course, El Cazador chose to stay in this hotel. Morgana had said he was stinking rich and travelling in class, and Captain Gringo had no idea what he *looked* like!

When Gaston came in to report he liked his big brass bedstead and just couldn't wait to fill it up with somebody softer than either of them, the tall American grimaced and said, "We'd better not cruise the lobby or tap room. We don't know what the guys after us look like. They know us on sight. Need I say more?"

"*Merde alors,* I wish you hadn't even said that! Why

are we paying two Yankee dollars a day for these rooms if they are not safe?"

Captain Gringo continued exploring his corner room and bath as he explained, "These *rooms* are the safest place I could think of—for now—because they should be the last place anyone would expect us to be, even if they were staying in this hotel. I said to go easy on the room service, not that we couldn't use it. If we have light meals sent up from the kitchen and use the money we save to overtip the help . . . oh, shit!"

"What's the matter?" asked Gaston as Captain Gringo stood in the doorway of the small adjoining bathroom. The tall American said, "There's a sink and commode, no tub or shower."

"Ah, *oui,* I noticed a sign down the hall pointing to the bathing facilities. I see what you mean. But a person sleeping alone does not have to worry much about his or her body odor. We can take discreet whore baths with our jolly little sinks, non?"

"I guess so. But nothing beats a couple of hot tubs a day to keep the mushrooms from sprouting in the parts you miss in the tropics. Okay, screw the hot tubs."

"What about hot women? There must be some ladies of joy working the best hotel in town, non?"

Captain Gringo started to object. But fair was fair and he couldn't say *he* wouldn't be buying it, when he was as old and gray around the edges as Gaston. The class of whores who worked grand hotels tended to be cool discreet pros who didn't talk about their clients without a damned good reason. He nodded at Gaston and said, "I don't have to tell you how to work something out with the bellhop. But if you have to, make sure you overtip everybody."

"Surely you jest! This is a hotel frequented by Englishmen, and as any waiter in Paris can tell you, the English are *très* lousy tippers. The people here should be overjoyed with even modest tips and you just said we had to be thrifty, non?"

"Overtip anyway. Since you can't hold out without extra room service, take good care of the hotel help and don't try to question the girl until you've sent for her twice."

"Now I know you are insane! Who ever heard of paying the same woman *twice* when one can have variety for the same fee? A business woman has to be *très fantastique* in bed to rate repeat orders, Dick."

"I know. That's why she ought to feel flattered. Jesus, Gaston, don't you know *anything* about making instant friends in a strange place?"

Gaston laughed and said, "Ah, oui, I begin to grasp the method in your madness. Whores do not tell tales on repeat customers. They might, on the other hand, tell tales *to* repeat customers. Very well, I shall butter up the local vice ring, as a brave duty to you. But what about your own amusements as we lay low like *le tar baby* in this mundane hotel for . . . how long?"

"Three or four days ought to do it. Don't worry about me. I'll catch up on my reading and make sure nobody busts in on you while you're playing slap and tickle across the hall."

"You're going to wind up playing with yourself."

"Hey, what can I tell you, *that* can be a novelty, too. I didn't check us in here for fun, and I didn't ask for top floor rooms because I wanted to pay extra for the trade winds. I've got a nice view of the harbor and you can watch the main plaza from your side if you can find the time for an occasional peek. El Cazador may arrive in a private yacht. If he comes by land with his private army, you may notice some activity in the plaza at paseo time. His hired guns are Mexican, not Honduran and . . ."

"I can spot the different species of hats from a distance," Gaston cut in, adding, "One of the reasons I scouted before approaching when I saw you with El Tigre was the hat and boots he had on. The locals have a more West Indian approach to costume. Let us get back to the *ladies* you are alloting me. I can't just ask even a friendly whore if El Cazador is staying at this hotel, can I?"

"Hardly, and make that *one* lady, singular. She doesn't have to tell you a hell of a lot, so don't ask a hell of a lot. Belize is not a tourist spa, so most of the guys staying here should be regulars and most of the strangers figure to be Englishmen. El Cazador might or might not check in under his right name, Roderico Montalban. Either way, a well-heeled Hispanic who's new in town ought to be noticed more than you and me around this hotel. I don't know exactly what he looks like, but Morgana says he's a charming good-looking Latin and Greystoke said he's a Basque, if that means anything."

Gaston nodded and said, "It does to me, if he has typical Basque features. They look more French than most Spaniards and more Spanish than most French. You still didn't tell me why you turned down Greystoke's offer, Dick. I know the son-of-a-camel can be tedious to work for, but I would prefer to be out in the field, well armed and backed by other British agents than cooped up here, waiting for the other shoe to drop."

"I turned him down for two reasons," Captain Gringo said. "It's not a good idea to let prospective clients think they can stiff you on a contract and then ask you to work for them again. But the kicker was that his new job called for a run north again into Mexico."

"But that's where El Cazador has his jolly hunting preserve!"

"I *said* I turned Greystoke down. Look, let's chew on the bone some more when we've both got something new to say. We're holed up safe for now, it's almost supper time, and I'm hungry. You want me to have room service send something up here for you, too?"

"*Mais non,* I prefer to dine alone and gaze out the other window. I also wish to have a private conversation with the hired help, my old and celibate."

So Captain Gringo waited until Gaston ducked into his own quarters across the hall before he used the house phone next to his own brass bedstead to call room service. They said they'd send someone up with a menu. They did. He'd been expecting a male waiter. The waitress who arrived was about eighteen and yummier than anything they could possibly be serving for supper.

In Brazil she'd have been considered a white girl with a dash of Negro blood. Naturally, in a British colony, she was considered a light nigger. She said her name was Daisy and her accent was Jamaican. She stood demure and apparently a little uneasy as he scanned the menu, added up the prices in his head, picked out the cheapest gut-fillers, and sent her on her way, resisting an impulse to pat her very tempting derriere as she turned to go. Her skirts hung down almost covering her trim ankles, of course, but the faded black cotton was thin and her derriere was shapely as hell.

While he waited, he stepped over to the window for another look at the harbor. He saw Greystoke's yacht was still there. The steamer taking Morgana home was of course long gone. A schooner with a black hull and chocolate brown sails was sailing into port with the trades. It had its fore and aft sails spread to either side to catch the wind from astern and somehow looked more like a big jungle bat than a vessel. He told himself not to be so dramatic. There was no law saying El Cazador was the only guy on the mosquito coast allowed to have a spooky-looking vessel.

Before the batlike schooner could do anything much out there, Daisy returned with his light supper on a rolling table. He paid her and added a sixpence tip. She seemed pleasantly surprised. He'd wanted her to be. He didn't want them gossiping downstairs about him being thrifty.

A guy who ate little but tipped right sounded like a guy who was simply a light eater, not a bum. Hotel staffs worried about things like that, even when you paid a couple of nights in advance. The pretty quadroon said she'd be back in an hour for the dishes and left. As he sat at the rolling table and ate, he judged from occasional sounds he heard that Gaston was being served by Daisy, too. He hoped Gaston had sense enough to behave himself. Exotic beauties like Daisy didn't have to work as waitresses if they were easy to get in a horizontal position. The pretty waitress looked and acted like a lady. He wondered what her story was. He knew he'd never know. It's not polite to ask a shy-looking, almost white girl how come she's almost white. He knew both blacks and whites tended to act superior to high yellows where she came from. Jamaican law forbade legal marriages between races. So while a black Jamaican as well as a white Jamaican could swear to being legitimate, girls like Daisy just didn't like to discuss their family tree.

It didn't take him long to finish. He hadn't ordered enough to spend an hour or even half an hour with. He lit a cigar and moved over to the window again. He saw the bat-winged schooner tied up and, what the hell, Greystoke's white-hulled steam yacht was now moving out to sea!

He blew a thoughtful smoke ring as he watched. Then he shrugged it off. Greystoke had said the Brits were up to something vile up Mexico way and he'd said he didn't want to play. So he had no right to feel left out. But he hadn't realized until now that he'd been subconsciously regarding Greystoke as an ace in the hole.

With the local head of British Intelligence gone, his fix with the colonial constabulary was shot, too. He and Gaston were on their own. The constabulary probably wasn't looking for them at the moment. But if they made any noise, all bets were off. Meanwhile, since both he and Gaston were wanted, dead or alive, El Cazador was free to gun them down like dogs and simply take a modest bow when the cops asked him why he'd been so unpleasant!

He rolled the table closer to the door for the waitress when she returned and muttered to himself, "Hey, let's not start whimpering in the dark. It's not dark yet. Nothing's going to happen right now."

Then, through the panels of the nearby door, he heard the crash of a falling dish and a familiar voice pleading, "Please, sir, I'm not that kind of girl!"

It was the waitress, Daisy. Had Gaston gone nuts? He swore under his breath and opened the door to see what the crazy old fart was up to. But Gaston's door across the hall was closed. A couple of doors down, Daisy was struggling in the arms of a very fat and very drunken slob. Captain Gringo knew better, but as Daisy cast an imploring glance his way he sighed and walked over to them. The drunk had at least a hundred pounds advantage on the petite quadroon, but she was ten times as sober so the struggle was about even until Captain Gringo stepped in and rabbit-punched the fat drunk from behind. The slob let go of Daisy, so she fell on her pretty butt as Captain Gringo caught the falling drunk under the arm pits, and muttered, "Steady, old chap" and dragged him into his room. The guy was out cold, so he didn't answer. Captain Gringo got him to his bed and rolled him aboard before he grabbed the portable table Daisy had made the mistake of rolling into his room and shoved it out in the hall ahead of him. As he kicked the door shut with the aid of his boot heel, he saw Daisy was on her feet again and that her face was as pale as it could get. He shot a glance along the hall doors behind her. At this hour most of the other guests seemed to be out, probably strolling in the sunset paseo or whatever. He smiled reassuringly at the pretty quadroon and said, "All's well that ends well. You'd better get this back to the kitchen, Daisy."

"You hit him!" she gasped, adding, "He's a very important regular guest, and when he tells them downstairs . . ."

"Hey, calm down. What's he going to tell them? I cold-cocked him from behind. If he remembers anything when he comes to, he'll think he passed out while he was acting like a jerk-off. He's still got his wallet. The door locks automatically. Trust me, Honey. I hardly ever clobber a slob without thinking ahead."

She looked more hopeful, albeit still frightened, as she said, "I thank you from the bottom of my heart, sir. You saw what he was trying to do. But if they question me at all . . ."

"Let's duck into my room a minute. This is no place to make battle plans."

He saw she was still rattled. So he took her arm and, rolling the drunk's room service table ahead of them, got them all under cover. The two tables tended to fill the space in the tiny room. So he sat her on the bed and stood by the door as he closed it behind him and said, "Look, the one dish that broke is on the hall rug. The guy who attacked you shouldn't remember a hell of a lot after leaving the tap room downstairs. If he does, I'll back you, okay?"

"You'll *what* me, sir? I don't understand. Why are you doing this for me?"

"Call it a tip. I've always been a big spender. When you take those tables down to the kitchen, say you served me but that the other guy never answered his door. That'll explain the uneaten food and they'll be mad at him, not you, for ordering a meal and not paying. If there's any argument, send the boss up to me and I'll say you gave me okay service and that I remember you disturbing me a little by pounding a lot on that other door. I'll remember going to my door, looking out, and seeing you leave after you couldn't get any answer. See how easy it works?"

She brightened and said, "Even I can manage a simple story like that. But the mess in the hall . . ."

He took an empty tea plate from his own table and put it on the drunk's before he said, "That was my fault. As you were leaving, I found an extra dish I'd forgot to put back on the table. You'd left. I put it on the floor just outside my door. Some careless guest must have stepped on it and the shards got sort of kicked along the rug, right? Oh, hell, just get back to the kitchen and let me worry about the busted china. I'll pick it up as soon as the coast is clear."

"You would do this, sir? You are a white Englishman!"

"Big deal. I know they wouldn't want you poor happy darkies to know this, Honey, but lily white Englishmen dig coal and work as garbage men in the old country. Come on, Daisy, it's going to take two trips to avoid comment and the sooner you get cracking, the less comment there'll be."

That did it. She leaped off the bed like she'd suddenly noticed it was a hot stove and, at his suggestion, took his empty service down the hall first at a rapid pace. He waited until she was out of sight, made sure nobody else was coming, and darted down to the drunk's door to scoop up the three shards of china. He went back to his own room and dropped them in his waste basket. As long as he was on his feet, he looked out the window. It was getting darker. Nothing else interesting was happening.

A while later, he heard someone pounding on another door. He didn't stick his head out and after a while the pounding stopped. He'd almost finished his cigar when Daisy came back. She was grinning like a kid who'd just swiped a bushel of apples and gotten away with it. As she closed the door behind her, she said, "It worked! The boss is very angry, but not at me! He went to Sir Ivor's room and when he didn't get an answer to his knock, he let himself in with his pass key. He says he found the fat idiot drunken into a stupor again. That is what he called Sir Ivor—a fat idiot!"

"Well, fair is fair, he *was* a fat idiot. So let's forget the whole mess, shall we?"

"I shall never forget what you did for me, sir," she sighed. "You see, I really need this job. So I don't know what I would have done if you hadn't come to my rescue."

He smiled gently down at her and said, "I'm sure you wouldn't have done what he wanted." So she blushed dusky rose and murmured, "Thank you. I'm not used to being treated like a woman of quality. I'm sure you must have noticed my complexion, and some people seem to think it's open season on girls like me."

"Some people are stupid as well as needlessly cruel. But speaking of open season, Daisy, I understand there's a famous hunter staying somewhere here in Belize. You wouldn't know if a Spanish Grandee named Montalban is a guest in this hotel, would you?"

She shook her head and said, "I don't remember anyone like that checking in recently, sir. You and that nice French gentleman across the hall are the only recent arrivals. Most of the guests have been here some time. Would you like me to ask around?"

"No thanks. But I'd sure appreciate it if you'd tell me about anyone asking if someone answering *my* description was staying here, Daisy."

"Heavens, is this Spanish gentleman an enemy of yours?"

He chose his words carefully before he answered. Daisy owed him a small favor. She didn't look like she harbored wanted criminals on a regular basis. So he kept his voice light as he said, "You might call it a one-sided affair of honor. You know how some guys are about women. This

Maldonado seems to think I, ah, flirted with his woman."

Daisy smiled, Mona Lisa-like, and asked, "Oh? And did you?"

"I never talk about a lady behind her back. Suffice it to say the jerk-off thinks I did. You must know how silly some Hispanics get if they even suspect such a thing."

"I certainly do. We have occasional guests from Mexico or Guatemala staying here. Don't worry, sir—one hand washes the other, as they say, and since you looked out for me, I'll look out for you."

She left with his rolling table. It wasn't until he snuffed out the cigar end in the ash tray that he saw she'd left his sixpence tip beside it. He sighed. Her pathetic little gesture touched him. Life had surely been rough on the sweet little quadroon if the small favor he'd done her meant that much to her.

He started to reach for another smoke. He decided not to. He had only so many cigars and a long lonely night ahead of him. It was getting quite dark now. The hotel had up-to-date Edison lamps, but he didn't turn them on. He'd forgotten to order the evening papers with his supper.

Early evening was always the most lonely time in a strange town, even when a knock-around guy was free to prowl. He knew that over in the plaza the paseo would have started. Any number of lonely native girls would be cruising under the plaza lamps in search of love with a discreet stranger. But he told himself to forget it. It wouldn't be discreet for him to look for a pick-up while El Cazador had picked him for current target practice! Besides, if he got really desperate, he could probably get laid the easy way, as Gaston suggested.

He rejected the unromantic notion. If a guy was going to be completely practical about his sex life, he was better off making love to his fist. But that didn't sound romantic, either. He decided to risk a run down to the newsstand in the lobby. Daisy had assured him nobody answering El Cazador's description was staying here. The maniac's trackers and beaters seemed to be Hispanics, too, so how much trouble could a guy get into just by buying a paper and perhaps some magazines and extra smokes? It was shaping up to be one of those nights calling for plenty of cigars and reading material.

The lobby downstairs was nearly deserted; but as he made his purchases at the newsstand near the desk, he noticed a voluptuous woman in widow's weeds and a big picture hat seated under a potted palm, like a black widow in a web. She was attractive, in a sort of spooky way. But he ignored her as he made his purchases and went back up to his room. He tossed the reading material and the box of claro cigars on the bed and stripped to give himself a quick whore bath with a wash cloth. Then he dried off and lay across the bed with a cigar in his teeth and the .38 near at hand as he lounged, naked, reading the papers.

Gaston's pointed answer to El Cazador's challenge had caused more of a local flap than they'd expected. It was on the front page, albeit reported all wrong, fortunately.

The constabulary had it down as a simple waterfront stabbing in the native quarter. They identified El Tigre as a nameless Latin passing through who'd run afoul of a couple of beach combers. The waiter at the café had described Gaston as another Latin, and himself as a hulking Swede or German derelict who needed a shave and a bath a lot.

Captain Gringo chuckled. El Cazador and his surviving lackeys would still know who El Tigre had run into, since El Cazador had sent him with the grotesque message in the first place. But the cops were looking for a couple of other guys.

He turned to the international news to see if he could get a line on what was up with Greystoke's bunch. He wasn't able to. The Cuban mess was heating up again. The exiled Cuban patriot, Tomás Estrada Palma, was still trying to direct an insurrection against the Spanish colonial government from his headquarters in New York. The new colonial governor, "Butcher" Weyler, was shoving Cubans in some new fangled device called a concentration camp. Nothing was going on in Yucatan right now. El Presidente Diaz didn't need concentration camps to keep Mexican rebels in line. His Rurales simply shot the poor bastards, regardless of age, sex, or political persuasion.

Captain Gringo knew British Intelligence wasn't out to overthrow the Mexican dictatorship. Washington wouldn't like it. Captain Gringo had found out the hard way that "big business" and the politicos they ran in the States considered the bloody handed Diaz something they called a "stable government." He'd never figured out why this was so great. But the Brits would get their wrists slapped by the U.S. Marines if they messed with either Mexico or Cuba, so what the hell could Greystoke be up to?

He heard a soft tap on his door but it wasn't Gaston's knock. He got up, wrapped a towel around his middle, picked up the gun, and switched off the lamp before he opened it a crack.

He'd been hoping it might be Daisy, even though he'd told himself not to dream the impossible. But it was the bigger, whiter dame in the picture hat and widow's weeds. She was alone, her hands were empty, so he let her in, saying, "Excuse my state of dishabille, Ma'am. I wasn't expecting guests."

She laughed, lightly, and said, "Certainly not respectable ones. You certainly have a nice pair of shoulders, Captain Gringo."

That took care of any ideas about throwing her out as a needless complication. He closed the door behind her and waved her to a seat on the bed with the muzzle of his revolver. There was enough light through the open window to see well enough without turning the lamp back on. He said, "Okay, first you strip and then we can talk."

"I *beg* your pardon!"

"Look, Toots, you came to me, I didn't approach you. Ladies who drop my professional name when I'm not registered under it make me nervous as hell. If you know who I am, you know why. So take off your duds and let me check a few things out. I mean, right now. This isn't a bunch of flowers I'm pointing at you."

"My God, would you shoot an unarmed woman?"

"No. So let's make sure you're an unarmed woman. Fold your clothes over the foot rail of that bed and don't make sudden movements with those hands until I decide whether we're going to be friends or enemies."

"Damn it, I'm not accustomed to being stripped on sight by strange men, Captain Gringo!"

"Welcome to the club. That's twice you've dropped my name in vain. You can tell me who you are as you undress, okay?"

"I think you really mean that! They told me you were ruthless, but really, I never expected *this*!"

"I'm alive, tonight, because I like to surprise people. Like I said, first we strip and then we talk. Since you know so much about me, I hope you know I'm a man of my word, and this is still a .38. So take off your Goddamn duds!"

She unpinned her hat, put it aside, and nervously began to fumble with the buttons of her black bodice as she murmured, "Are you going to rape me?"

He shrugged and said, "Rape is in the eye of the rapee. It's seduction if she enjoys it. But don't worry, I don't know if I have hard feelings for you either way, right now. I only know I'm on the run and, like I said, nervous. By the way, are you a Basque?"

"Why, yes, how did you know?"

"Something a little French birdie told me. You look too French to be Spanish and too Spanish to be French. Do you have a name?"

"I am called Ynez Bilbao y Viscaya and, as you guessed, my people have been important in the Basque regions since Roman times," she replied, standing up to finish taking off her black dress. That left her wearing black silk stockings, a black lace teddy, and a tightly cinched black corset. He decided she must like black. She stood facing him, hands on rather ample hips, as she asked, "There, are you satisfied?"

He said, "No. You can leave the corset and socks on. But I want a look at your lap."

"Oh, you're horrid!" she gasped. "You can see I'm not carrying concealed weapons, damn it!"

He cocked an eyebrow as he ran his gaze over her pneumatic curves. Then he said, "Well, it'd have to be a small one. Just show me that you're a woman and I'll be satisfied, for now."

Ynez laughed incredulously and pulled the silken crotch of her teddy up, folded into the slit between her legs as she said, "Really, I've never been asked to prove my sex before! What on earth did you take me for, a female impersonator?"

"The thought crossed my mind. A soft good-looking Basque I don't know on sight has been talking silly, and everyone says he's nuts. No offense, but you're at least five nine, so about that final reassurance . . ."

"Listen, I can't get this teddy off without removing my corset and I need help with that, too. Would you, ah, settle for just feeling?"

He said that sounded fair enough and stepped closer, reaching for her with the hand he wasn't holding the gun in. Since he had been holding the towel with it, the towel fell to the rug between them as he reached out, slid his fingers inside her thin black silk underwear, and explored her invisible genitals with his fingers. She flinched and took a startled hop backward as he ran his fingers up into her moist interior. She fell sideways across the bed as she sobbed, "That was dirty! You could have told I was a girl without putting your nasty fingers all the way in!"

He picked up the towel, wiped his hands on it, and sat beside her with it across his lap as he said, "You'd be surprised how many ladies carry a loaded derringer there. But, okay, I can see you're unarmed and female. Start talking."

She sat up, saying, "The first thing I want to say is *no*! You're not fooling me with the calm clinical tone. I was once a happily married woman and I couldn't help noticing that semi-erection when you dropped the towel!"

"Hey, don't take it personal. It always does that when I'm alone with a beautiful woman. You did have something *else* to talk about, didn't you?"

"I certainly did. But I never expected to discuss it half naked in the dark with a sex maniac. Good heavens, I don't know where to begin."

"Start with what you were going to say before I checked you out."

"Very well. I want you to kill a man for me. I understand you're very good at that."

"I'm a soldier of fortune, not a hired assassin. Who sent you?"

"I promised not to tell. Suffice it to say, another woman you once did similar favors for. She warned me about that awfully dangerous looking other weapon of yours too. Is that enough to convince you it was an old friend of yours?"

He laughed, "It doesn't sound like an enemy. Okay, I know how friends of friends swear one to silence. Get to the fun part. Who do you want knocked off? But, before you tell me, I want it understood I don't accept simple murder contracts."

"Aren't you using Jesuit logic, Captain Gringo? They say you wiped out a whole infantry brigade with machine-gun fire just a few months ago."

He shrugged and said, "Yeah, you're probably right. But a guy has to draw the line somewhere. They call me a renegade as well as a hired gun. But I like to think of myself as a professional soldier. It's like calling less bloody violence seduction instead of rape, I guess. My sidekick says I'm picky, too. But I just don't like straight assassination. Now, if you had an *army* for me to take on . . ."

"How does a large and dangerous gang sound?"

"Much better. What's the score? You're having bandit problems around de old plantation?"

"I don't have the plantation anymore. El Cazador stole that, too, after killing my husband!"

He blinked in surprise and said, "That must have smarted. How come you seem to be still around, Ynez?"

"I was home in Spain, visiting my people, when it happened. So I don't know the details. I haven't been brave enough to return to Quintana Roo, alone. You see, El Cazador is also a Basque, so I knew all about him from friends and neighbors back home. All I know for certain about my husband's death is that the Mexican authorities accepted it as a hunting accident. My poor Carlos disliked El Cazador and never would have accepted an invitation to his hunting party. We had heard very odd things about his hunting parties. But when I tried to tell this to the Mexican envoy to Madrid, he said I was behaving hysterically. You see, Roderico Montalban is very powerful in Quintana Roo and . . ."

"Never mind that part," he cut in, adding, "I already know El Cazador is a spoiled rich kid who's allowed to shoot less important people. He's after me, too. Never mind why. That's a long story, too. Do you know the nut, personally?"

"Of course. When my late husband and I first cleared our land in Mexico he was a frequent visitor and, unfortunately, we both found him rather charming, at first."

"Yeah, another lady already told me he doesn't tell you he's a homicidal maniac right up front. I gotcha. You and your husband socialized with him long enough to start thinking it wasn't such a hot idea. Then, while you were away, he turned on Señor Bilbao, got his friends in high places to transfer your land titles to his, and so forth."

"Why, that's *exactly* what happened! In Madrid, they told me my husband owed El Cazador a huge gambling debt and that the I.O.U. he produced seemed valid and . . ."

"Never mind the easy stuff. Tell me about El Cazador's looks and personality. You'd still have your clothes on if I knew what he looked like for sure. He was described to me as a soft sort of effeminate gent of middle height—for a man—and since I know for a fact he doesn't sleep a lot with women, the idea that he could sneak up in drag wasn't as wild as it might sound."

Ynez reclined, more relaxed, on one elbow as she nodded and said, "I met his wife, a rather common English girl. I never got to know her well. But I gathered she was unhappy with her Roderico."

"She was. He was either a mariposa or had no interest in sex either way. Some monomaniacs are like that."

"Really? Morgana Montalban told you her husband was a degenerate? When did you meet her?"

"Never mind. Last I heard she'd left him and died or something. Describe the guy to me, damn it!"

"Poor thing, he must have killed her, too. Let me see, you're right about him being my height, now that I think of it. I suppose all of us Basques look enough like relatives to be taken as such by outsiders. Though I assure you neither the Bilbao nor Viscaya clans are related to the witch folk."

"Which witch folk are we talking about?" he asked with a puzzled frown. She smiled sadly and said, "That's right, you're not a Basque. Most of us have been good Christians, since the creed was forced upon us in the middle ages. But the wilder Montalban tribe remained pagan long after the rest of my people accepted salvation. During the Inquisition they burned a lot of Montalbans. Those who survived say, today, have also seen the light. But the old ones whisper that in the high hidden dells of our ancient mountains, where the oak and pine still grows . . ."

"Gotcha. He comes from a spooky family, too. Okay, no offense, but I'm starting to picture him as a guy who looks like he's related to you. I keep painting a pouty expression on his soft face. No good?"

"No good. Roderico is about thirty, does have a heart-shaped Basque face like mine, and seems boyish and charming when you meet him."

"What does he look like when he's shooting at you?"

"Nobody knows. He's said to be a crack shot. So there have been no survivors to gossip about his other moods. Since we agree he's insane, I imagine he would appear rather frightening at such times. On the other hand, since he's mad, he may smile *then* too!"

Captain Gringo frowned thoughtfully and growled, "He's not the main problem. A spoiled brat who's bored with shooting birds would be dead by now if he didn't have a private army of trackers and beaters to give him the edge over those he hurts. If I take the job, what kind of money are we talking about, Doll?"

"I will give you a thousand dollars, U.S. It is all I have."

He shook his head. "Forget it, then," he said. "I couldn't possibly take on the job for that."

She leaned forward, brushing his naked chest with a silk clad nipple as she pleaded, "Please, Captain Gringo.

I would do anything for you if you would help me! It's more than revenge. He stole my land. He's a disgrace to our people. He's a monster who must be killed!"

He didn't push her away as she wriggled closer. It felt too good. But he said, "Hey, the price for me and Gaston is not the problem. I'd shoot the bastard for you for free, even without the bonus you'd better back out of while the backing's good."

She moved even closer and ran a silk-sheathed leg between his as she pleaded, "I don't want to back away. I have feelings, too. Please say you'll do it for me, Captain Gringo!"

He took her in his arms. "It depends on just what you want me to do for you," he stated. "I can't go up against a private army without the money to buy some weapons and help. A lot more weapons and help than we could swing on a lousy thou. As for anything *else* I can do for you, if you don't watch that hand of yours, you know damned well what I'll do!"

She didn't heed his warning. She wrapped her cool fingers around his throbbing shaft and proceeded to stroke it skillfully as she moaned, "I have nobody else to turn to, Captain Gringo!"

"Hell," he said, "you may as well start calling me Dick, if we're going to be informal."

Then he kissed her and rolled her on her back to let his own free hand roam at will. She responded eagerly to his kissing and tongued him with skill as well as passion. After that it got a little complicated. She still had the damned corset on, and while some teddys opened at the crotch with a snap, hers didn't.

He had to shove the lacy silk to one side as he mounted her. She gasped as he entered her. He believed her story about being a widow some time as he ran it to the roots in her trembling moist flesh. After the repeated, totally nude, daylight orgies with the earthy Morgana and Pepita, it made a welcome contrast to make love in semi-darkness to a perfumed woman almost, but not quite, shielded by smooth clean silk and piquant scratchy lace. Her inner thighs felt creamy nude against his hips as she hugged him with her silk-sheathed lower limbs locked across his naked buttocks. Her corset formed an asexual barricade between their bellies, adding somehow to the softness of her silk clad breasts against his heaving chest.

But enough was enough and so once they'd both climaxed, hard and fast, they both agreed it would be nicer with her completely stripped. So she took off every stitch and when he mounted her again, it felt like she was a brand new woman, even hotter than before. There was more to it than the change in costume. Once she'd gotten over her initial shyness as well as her underwear, Ynez let herself go like the sex starved widow she said she was.

Captain Gringo wasn't half as hard up. But he had no trouble keeping up with her. She seemed willing to do most of the work. Her breasts were bigger and softer than Morgana's and of course much lighter than Pepita's. So they made an inspiring novel sight as she bounced them, and everything else she had, after getting on top. He tried to hold back, but as she skillfully milked another ejaculation out of him with her whole body, she laughed, "I felt that. Do you mind if I don't stop just yet? I'm almost there, too!"

"Be my guest!" he said. So by the ime she collapsed atop him moaning in orgasm he was inspired again. He rolled her over to do it right as she sobbed, "Oh, God, not again!"

"Hey," he laughed, "in bed you don't have to be so formal. Just call me Dick."

She got it and giggled as he pounded them both to glory again. But then he made the tactical error of rolling off for a breather and a smoke. She shared the claro with him as they lay dreamily in each other's arms for a tender time. Then she sighed and replied, "I must leave soon, Dick. I am staying at a private home here in Belize with distant Basque relations. It must be at least ten and I have my reputation to think of."

"Come on, Doll, it's early even for the stuffy rules down here. I don't meet many Grandee types, but I've gotten many a Spanish girl after midnight and nobody turned us into pumpkins."

"Basque girls don't turn into pumpkins at midnight, Dick. They turn into fallen women if they start coming home without an escort after sunset, and you may have noticed it's long after sunset. The people I'm staying with are sweet, but I sometimes think they consider Queen Victoria a loose-living woman!"

"In that case I'd better escort you home," he said, then he wondered why the hell he'd said a dumb thing like that. She said, "Well, they do have a telephone. Perhaps if I called and told them I'd met an old friend."

He didn't want to take that chance, either. But Ynez rolled atop him, reaching across for the telephone on the end table, and it felt sort of nice as she lay there with her breasts against him while she gave the switchboard operator a number, waited, and proceeded to make funny noises. He'd heard Basque before. Nobody but a Basque understood a word of it. Basque wasn't at all related to either Spanish or French and the only part he was able to figure out was that they sure liked the letters S and K a lot. He started strumming on her derriere like a soft banjo as she prattled on with someone at the other end who must have understood her, impossible as that seemed. Then she hung up and said, "I still have to leave soon. My hostess says she's worried about me."

"Okay, just one more, then."

"Wait, Dick, we still haven't settled the matter I originally came to see you about. We've been coming too much to talk about it."

He got his hand between the cheeks and she opened her thighs as she lay across him as he said, while fingering her, "You can tell I wouldn't tell you to get this pretty tail back to Spain unless there was a damned good reason, Doll. But your idea is crazy. I don't enjoy playing *Run Rabbit Run* and it sure would feel good to turn the tables on El Cazador. But a pro has to know, and taking on a maniac with a private army, and the Mexican Rurales on his side as well, would make *me* a maniac, too!"

"Listen, Dick, many of the local peones hate and fear El Cazador. I am sure I could get the workers on our stolen plantation to help and . . ."

"And then what would we have: a mob of barefoot boys with cheeks of tan against a sadistic killer and his professional gun slingers? Be serious, Honey buns. I'm armed at the moment with a .38 revolver, period!"

"But don't you have a machinegun, Dear? They told me you used a machinegun."

"I do, when I have one handy. Did you think I carried a machinegun around in my pocket, Ynez? Soldiers-of-fortune hire out to armies. They don't keep one on them."

"What if I bought you a machinegun? Oh, that feels good."

"I've already added up what you and the two of us have together, and it's just not enough to mount a serious expedition. Roll over and let me put the real thing in that sweet little jelly roll."

So they didn't talk for a while, and when they were done she insisted she really had to go home. He'd been afraid she'd say a dumb thing like that. On the other hand, it might be dangerous for her to spend the whole night. The staff was sure to gossip about an Hispanic woman of quality having breakfast in a single, paid for by a quiet gentleman who didn't go out much. It was probably safe enough to run her home, too. It was dark as hell out and she hadn't said she wanted him to take her to the opera.

They washed up, got dressed, and he told her to sit tight as he checked a few things. She giggled and said she doubted if she'd feel tight again for a while. He saw nobody in the hall. He ducked across, rapped on Gaston's door, and when the Frenchman opened it a crack, he said, "I'm going out a while."

Gaston said, "*Eh bien,* in that case I shall go back in a while. Her name is Maranza and she says there are other girls at home like her. Do you want me to ask her to fix you up?"

"Too late. I've been fixed beyond common duty. I'll check with you later."

Gaston closed his door. Captain Gringo opened his again and got Ynez. Together they went down the back steps and out a side entrance. She had to lead. She said they were headed for the Spanish enclave of the old native quarter. You couldn't prove it by him, after they'd gone a few blocks. Apparently the British colonial office didn't think anyone but white people who spoke English rated street lamps.

As in most neighborhoods inhabited by Hispanic types, there wasn't a hell of a lot to see, anyway. The introverted stucco homes presented blank walls and an occasional doorway or loop hole to the narrow winding street. As his eyes adjusted to the dark he took bearings on the few landmarks, to keep from getting lost on the way back. He didn't want to have to ask directions.

They passed an old baroque church with its oaken door ajar, spilling a trip-wire of golden light across the cobbles. Beyond, the street bottle-necked through an archway and ran dark as a mine shaft toward a distant pinpoint of light. Ynez said that was the doorway they were headed for. It figured. The doorways on either side had no lights over them.

As they moved arm-in-arm toward the distant tiny light, it winked off and on. Ynez didn't notice. Most people wouldn't have. But most people weren't Captain Gringo. So he shoved the Basque girl into a deeply recessed doorway and flattened out against her, drawing his. 38, as the machinegun aimed their way opened up, filling the narrow passage with stacatto noise and flame!

Ynez might have been screaming; it was hard to tell, as he shielded her with his body while the gun crew hosed the muzzle back and forth from maybe a hundred feet away. The jerk-offs were firing blindly since the calle was filled with blue gunsmoke even when the muzzle blasts illuminated the area like an Edison bulb flicking on and off. The gunner burned up the whole belt in one long burst that didn't really take as long as it sounded. Then the gun fell silent for the moment.

He heard the snickersnee of someone opening the action to insert a new belt. He didn't want them to insert a new belt. So he stepped out of the doorway and charged, firing his .38 blindly but sure they had to be somewhere between the pavement and that light one of them had been dumb enough to outline his head against.

By the time he got close enough to make out a Maxim squatting on its tripod mount, he could see the bodies sprawled just beyond it. He heard Ynez's shoe heels running toward him. He turned and said, "Keep going! Don't stop 'til you make it to your friends!"

She gasped as she spotted the bodies. But she didn't stop. He'd trained her to co-operate with him in every way. As he saw she was going to make it to the light at the end of the tunnel, he picked up the Maxim and an ammo box and headed the other way on the double. He left the mount behind, but they had managed to reload, just before he shot them up, so the long ammo belt was trailing behind him as he dashed out through the archway, heard a tinny police whistle ahead, and ran into an old church with the heavy weapon cradled in his arms like a big lethal foundling.

The nave seemed deserted. Light came from a rack of votive candles down near the altar. He slipped sideways into a pew, dropped to his knees and shoved the still warm mass of gun metal under the seats. Then he took off his hat and bowed his head. The cops might buy a blond head praying or they might not. What the hell, it was a British colony and he could always say he was Irish.

The door behind him thudded shut with an ominous finality. A soft voice said, "We must close now, my son. There seems to be violence in the night and, as you see, all my pobrecitos have gone home after vesper prayers."

Captain Gringo got to his feet, kicking the end of the ammo belt under the seats with his toe as he faced the old priest and said, "Out of respect for your cloth, I don't want to lie to you, Padre. So I'll ask right out if your custom of Sanctuary extends to people who might not be Catholic."

The old priest murmured, "Sanctuary is not a *custom* of my Faith, my son. It is the *law*. Sometimes those who enforce other laws have a hard time understanding this. But unless you are a relapsed heretic or a satanist, I must help you as best I can. How may I be of service to you, my son?"

"I'm not sure. I think I just need time to figure out a few moves. I'm not a satanist. I know what *that* is. I was baptized a Protestant. Does that make me a heretic in your eyes, Padre?"

"Of course not. The Church no longer regards honest Jews or Protestants as heretics. You are considered brothers, living, for now, in Invincible Ignorance."

"For now, Padre?"

"Of course. Human life is mayfly short, and you shall have eternity to chuckle at your doubtless well-meant but confused theology, once it's all explained to you properly in Heaven. I regret to say that in less enlightened ages certain followers of the True Faith confused a merely ignorant heretic with a relapsed heretic. But *they* were acting in error, too. You see, the inquisitors had distinct orders that only a person who renounced his or her heresy and accepted communion as a Catholic, and then went back on the agreement, to become a heretic a *second time*, was to be punished."

"You mean if I joined a monastery or something and then ran away, you'd call me a lapsed heretic, Padre?"

"No, my son, we'd call you a poor confused soul. It happens all the time. Since you are obviously from the British end of Belize, perhaps I'd better assure you we black papists haven't burned anyone at the stake for quite some time. But, by the way, the last witch executed by *Protestants* died in 1725. In fairness, it was in a remote Scottish village at the hands of a fanatic congregation. But some of our more enthusiastic inquisitors ignored orders from Rome, too."

The door opened and a couple of black constables stood in the doorway. One of them asked, in English, "Have you seen anybody ducking in here, Padre Junipero?" and the priest looked absolutely astonished.

He called back, "My young friend, here, and I have just been having a theological discussion. I can assure you nobody *else* has come in. May I ask what has happened, my son?"

"Gunfight, Padre Junipero. Looks like a couple of mean-looking thugs were laying for another down the calle a block."

"Oh, that must have been the shots we heard. I'm no expert on such matters, but it certainly sounded like what I've always imagined one of those new machinegun things should sound."

"You imagined right, Padre. There's spent brass all over the place and the tripod's still there. I don't know who they fired a whole belt of machinegun ammo at, but he surely must be a man not to mess with! The one witness willing to talk says he just walked into their muzzle flash and popped 'em both off with a bitty pistol! Ain't that something?"

Captain Gringo started to ask a foolish question, but bit his tongue. If the witness had things that screwed up, he hadn't seen anything, and he didn't want to explain his accent to a couple of nice enough cops who weren't even looking at him as they questioned the priest.

Padre Junipero made the sign of the cross and said, "If two men have been shot, it's my duty to give them last rites. Would you be good enough to wait for me here, my son? That way I shan't have to lock up and I ought to be back in a short while, as soon as things settle down, if you follow my meaning."

Captain Gringo did, and since the veiled message had been in Spanish, the two black cops couldn't have.

As the old priest followed the cops outside, Captain Gringo sat back down and concentrated on looking pious, with his heels against the machinegun under the seat. He couldn't move the damned thing back any further and somebody was sure to wonder what they were kicking under there at Morning Mass. Or were they? If he could somehow get a tarp to wrap it in and smuggle it into the hotel . . . Sure, the maid would think it was a camera or something. There *was* no safe place at the hotel to hide so much hardware, and what the hell did he want with it, anyway? He'd grabbed it mostly to keep anybody else from shooting it again. Now that he was maybe to first base—with who knew how many bases to go—the Maxim might just cause him more trouble than it was worth if he dragged it along any farther. A machinegun was a lot like a dame. They could both slow down a man on the run, but, boy, when you needed either, there was nothing like the real thing!

Padre Junipero returned sooner than the tall American expected. The old priest shut and bolted the door firmly behind him before he rejoined Captain Gringo and said, "The ambulance had already taken them away. One can only hope their souls are at rest. I think you had better stay here and keep me company for a while longer, Captain Gringo. There are still a lot of constables puttering about the scene of your latest brush with the dark angel."

"You know who I am, Padre?"

"Of course. One hears things in the confessional. When I heard the gunfire I ran outside. You didn't see me as you charged into my church holding that machinegun in your arms. But I saw you, and I recalled the stories told about you by the *pobrecitos*. As a man of the cloth I can hardly condone some of the methods you have used to right certain wrongs along the mosquito coast. On the other hand, I saw no reason to betray a young man who, in his own way, seems to have answered a few prayers."

Captain Gringo laughed weakly with relief and said, "You're all right, Padre Junipero. I'm sorry I didn't see right off that you were smarter than I thought. I'd better tell you what just happened out there."

"I wish you wouldn't. I don't believe your own faith recognizes the sanctity of the confessional and I do so hate to lie to the police. I know who and what you are. Don't tell me any more, unless there is some way I can help you further."

"You're pushing past nice guy into sainthood, Padre! But, okay, you already know about the machinegun, right?"

"Of course, you put it under that seat you're sitting on. I don't think you ought to leave it there."

"Neither do I. But could you hide it somewhere else, here, for me?"

"Oh, Dear me, we *are* stretching the laws of Sanctuary, my son! Could you give me a reason, without burdening me too greatly with guilty knowledge?"

"I've got more than one reason, Padre. I might or

might not want to use it myself. I certainly don't want it falling into the wrong hands. You see, there's this maniac after me who thinks I stole his wife and . . ."

"Stop right there, my son! It's enough that you are who and what you are. The *pobrecitos* have told me some of the things you have done for them with a machinegun in the past. As a man of God I must warn you: killing is a sin. As a man of humble birth, I know all too well how many tyrants need killing in Central America. Let us take ourselves and the weapon to my quarters and share a little bread and wine before you leave. Nobody will look for machineguns under *my* bed, I assure you!"

Captain Gringo laughed and dug the Maxim out, picked it up and followed Padre Junipero along a side aisle leading to the rectory. The situation seemed to tickle Padre Junipero's funny bone, too. He said, "I hope the Bishop never finds out about this. He might not understand that in Robin Hood's England, everyone was still Catholic."

Captain Gringo laughed again and said, "Hey, come to think of it, old Robin *must* have been! Welcome to the Greenwood, Friar Tuck!"

"Heavens, I'm too old and skinny to be Friar Tuck. Even though I am beginning to see how he must have felt about his outlaw congregation!"

Captain Gringo got back to the hotel with no further adventures, knocked the high sign on Gaston's door, and ducked into his own room. He sat on the bed, lit another smoke, and stared at the telephone on the end table, trying to remember the number Ynez had previously given the operator. He decided to skip it. Their relationship or whatever had been broken up a little early as well as very rudely. But he knew she'd made it to safety and if she was worried about him she could call him. For all he knew, she had. He started to pick up the phone to ask the switchboard downstairs if there were any messages. Then he gave himself a mental kick. That would be a swell move for a guy who'd *never left the hotel* tonight, right? He waited a while and then took out his watch. It was still on the prim and proper side of midnight, strange as that seemed. On the other hand, maybe Ynez figured late night calls to men weren't such good ideas, either. She'd probably call in the morning, if she called at all. He'd told her he didn't want to work for her. Maybe she'd just go looking for some other knock-around guy. He tried not to feel jealous about that. Any other soldier-of-fortune ready and willing to take on El Cazador doubtless deserved a good lay, too.

Gaston signaled against the door panels of Captain Gringo's room and was let in, stark naked and smoking his own cigar. As he straddled a chair, Captain Gringo frowned and said, "Couldn't you at least wrap a towel around your ass before you wandered around out in the hall?"

Gaston shrugged and said, "It's late and nobody saw me. But what if they did? It pays to advertise, non? But enough about my charms, Dick. I have an excited young thing waiting across the hall with an expressed desire to learn more about French culture. What exciting things have you been up to?"

Captain Gringo told him the whole story. Gaston whistled and said, "You *have* been a busy boy! Didn't your mother ever tell you never to follow Spanish speaking girls down dark alleyways, Dick?"

"I've considered that. The ambush looked more like it was set up for her, not me. They had no way of knowing in advance she'd be coming home with me and if I hadn't shoved her out of the way they'd have hosed her down with the same stream of automatic fire. Besides, Ynez is a Basque, not a cha-cha-cha I picked up in a cantina in Juarez."

Gaston grimaced and said, "Cantina girls are safer. Do you remember when the Moors and Christians were fighting over Spain, Dick?"

"I must have been on the Cape that summer. What about it?"

"The Basques fought both sides. Ditto when Napoleon invaded Spain. By then the Basque mountaineers had rifles, too. They sniped at Spaniards, French, and the English troops of Wellington. Apparently they regarded all outsiders as enemies. She lied about the so-called Basque names she threw at you. *Bilbao* and *Viscaya* are not family names. They are places. Real Basque clan names are long and unpronounceable."

"Couldn't that be why they use the towns they come from with outsiders? Jews in the middle ages used place names in their dealings with gentiles. Goldberg and Lowenstein are German towns, not Hebrew tribes. El Cazador calls himself Montalban and that's a white mountain in the Basque country, right?"

Gaston made a fly-brushing motion and said, "Forget what all these *très* mysterious neolithics call themselves, Dick. The really unsettling part is that if *one* Basque were able to track you to this hotel, another who prides himself on his hunting ability may have done so, too, non?"

Captain Gringo frowned and said, "Yeah, I already thought of that. If El Cazador had this address already, they'd have had the machinegun set up just outside, instead of closer to the place Ynez is staying. But it's probably only a question of time. According to Padre Junipero, around here I'm more famous than I thought."

"So when do we check out, and where do we run from here?"

"We'd better sleep on it. I can't think of a better place

to fort up. Even if El Cazador knows we're here, he'd be dumb to come after us in a respectable hotel filled with 'lime juicers.' The colonel government wouldn't like it."

"Have you considered that the dead-or-alive papers posted on us gives the son-of-a-camel a hunting permit, anywhere he finds us?"

"Sure. We could call the cops, if he didn't have a legal right to gun us. But that's where the other guests in this hotel come in. The law on both sides of the border know El Cazador's home address. So he wouldn't want to risk shooting anybody that *isn't* wanted dead or alive. The asshole just down the hall is a Sir. There are doubtless other important Brits staying here. He'd be dumb as hell to smoke up this posh hotel when he knows that sooner or later we have to leave it! Leaving at night could be dangerous for one's health. So our best bet would be broad daylight, with the streets all around crowded with innocent bystanders, see?"

"I have checked out of hotels before. Get to the part about where we go next, Dick."

"That's what I want to sleep on. I'm stuck. Even if we made it out of town and lost his trackers in the woods, too many people know we rest up between jobs in Costa Rica."

"Ah, but in Costa Rica the police are on *our* side, Dick!"

Captain Gringo shook his head and said, "Not really. We're not wanted in Costa Rica and the cops in San José are easy going. But those dead or alive wants apply anywhere, and a guy who can afford to go all the way to Africa to shoot elephants and natives can sure as hell afford to follow us to Costa Rica or, come to think of it, anywhere else in the world!"

Gaston groaned and said, "I wish you hadn't said that. You just spoiled my erection, and I worked so hard to get it up, too! What if we made a feint for Costa Rica and went back to Brazil? We have friends in Brazil, and it has a lot of trees to hide behind, hein?"

"El Cazador is expecting us to make a run for it. He's expecting us to run south, no matter where we're running. Let's think about that. If you were hunting a couple of guys you knew had friends to the south, you'd try to head them off that way, right?"

"Perhaps. But we are dealing with a lunatic who might do anything. If I was after someone I would not warn them in advance that I intended to kill them."

"Yeah, I've been thinking about that, too. Everyone agrees El Cazador's a sadistic monomaniac, but he's supposed to be a hell of a hunter, too. I think he sent El Tigre to flush us, not to give us a sporting chance."

"*Eh bien,* consider me flushed. But if I follow your twisted logic, you are assuming he is trying to make us leave town in a hurry. It sounds like a good idea to me, too. But what's *his* point?"

"That's the part I'm working on. As I said, a so-called responsible citizen has a perfect right to gun wanted outlaws on sight, anywhere he spots them. He had us spotted before he sent El Tigre to play *Tu Madre* with us. He didn't even have El Tigre covered, like the poor slob said. It must have disappointed the hell out of El Tigre when we didn't panic and run, too. The point is that El Cazador is afraid to blow us away here in British Honduras. That's an interesting point to ponder."

Gaston shook his head and said, "It works another way. Take him at face value as a sadist who enjoys cat and mouse. He wasn't at all reluctant to machinegun that woman tonight, Dick!"

"I noticed. He must have Ynez down as an enemy, too, since she says he murdered her husband and she's running around trying to recruit an army against him. You're right, he didn't mess around with old Ynez. Yet he plays games with us. There's more to this than meets the eye."

"Merde, I have a crazy dame across the hall, and if I don't get back to her she'll fall asleep on me. If he can't gun us here in British Honduras for some reason, our best bet is to just stay in British Honduras, non?"

"That could be a ploy, too. Greystoke's gone and we have no fix with the law, here. What if El Cazador's game is to keep us here until somebody *else* shows up?"

"Sacre Goddamn. You make a chess game out of *les checkers!* This is all too *fatigue*. Since we don't expect another attempt against us here in this hotel tonight, I must return to the front. Or perhaps her back. We have not tried that, yet."

When Gaston left, Captain Gringo made sure his door was locked, then undressed and got in bed. He tried to read. It didn't work. He kept running all that had happened through his mind over and over again, trying to find the pieces that fit into some rational pattern. But how did a guy make sense of a maniac's hobby?

He switched off the light. It took him another hour or so of thinking in circles before he must have fallen asleep. He knew he'd been asleep when he awoke at dawn, sat up wtih a frown and cocked his head, wondering what had awakened him. He heard it again. Somcone had a key in his lock and was gently, ever so gently, turning it.

The pretty quadroon called Daisy wasn't wearing her waitress uniform as she tip-toed into Captain Gringo's room but a flower print kimono and she'd let her long hair down. She gave a little gasp as the tall American, who'd flattened out against the wall by the door, gun in hand, grabbed her from behind, shoved the muzzle of the .38 against her floating rib, and kicked the door shut behind them with his bare heel. He manhandled her over to the bed, threw her across it, and patted her down for concealed weapons as she struggled to twist out from under him, protesting in a whisper that she was on his side. He didn't feel any concealed weapons, but everything else was swell. She was smaller, softer, and more rounded than the last lady he'd just been on top of. As he rolled her over, her kimono fell open. She was darker, too. He said, "Talk!" and Daisy said, "I came to warn you! There are some police inspectors in the building asking about you. I was in the kitchen, just ready to go on duty, and . . ."

"Is that why you're dresesd for bed, Daisy?"

"Of course. They didn't speak to me. If they noticed me at all as they spoke with the chef, they should remember me as just another colored girl in a waitress uniform. I slipped up, dashed up to my quarters in the garret, and changed."

"Gotcha. What happens when you're missed?"

"I asked another Jamaican girl who hadn't dressed yet to cover for me with the hotel. I'm allowed to be sick if I don't ask to be paid on the days I don't work. The police are asking everyone if you went out last night. So far, they haven't found anyone on the staff who can say one way or the other. They'll be knocking on that door any minute. Get off and let me get between the sheets, sir!"

He rolled off, suddenly feeling very naked in the dawn light. Daisy slipped off her kimono, looking naked indeed for a moment before she had herself demurely covered with the top sheet. He sat there, frowning down at her, and said, "Look, I can make up the lost pay to you. But why are you going out on such a long limb for me, Daisy?"

"You helped *me*, didn't you, sir?"

"Not *this* much! And you may as well call me Dick, now."

"Are you sure you don't mind my being so familiar, sir?"

"I'd say we certainly ought to look like we're on familiar terms, Daisy," he laughed. "But aren't you liable to get fired if you're caught in bed with a guest?"

"I don't know. I've never been caught in bed with anyone before."

Before they could discuss the matter further, there was an imperious knock on the door. Daisy's eyes got big as saucers. Captain Gringo rose, wrapped a towel around his middle, and hid the gun against his gut as he asked, "Who is it?"

"Constabulary, on Her Majesty's business, sir."

He opened the door with a puzzled frown pasted across his face. A brace of detectives in linen suits stood there. One asked politely if they could come in. He stepped back and waved them in with his free hand, asking sarcastically if he had any choice. The one who seemed to be in charge smiled pleasantly and answered, "Hardly, but we like to keep things as civilized as possible." He spotted the pretty quadroon in Captain Gringo's bed and said, "Good morning, miss," without batting an eye.

Captain Gringo sat on the bed with the cold metal of the .38 resting on his genitals under the towel as he waved them to seats. They remained standing. The spokesman said, "This should only take a moment, sir. May we ask where you were at about eleven last night?"

Captain Gringo placed a casual hand on Daisy's naked shoulder and said, "That's a dumb question. Where was I supposed to be?"

"That's what we're trying to determine, Mister, ah, Baxter. You did register downstairs as a Canadian named Baxter, didn't you?"

"Yeah, do you want to see my passport?"

"I'm sure it's in order, sir. Certain friends of yours in high places told us not to question your papers as long as you behaved yourself here in British Honduras for the moment. The question is how well you've been behaving. Last night a gentleman answering your description was seen leaving the scene of a gunfight with a smoking machinegun in his arms. Our roundsmen found a couple of dead men precariously close to the scene. We don't approve of people being machinegunned in the streets of Belize, Captain . . . uh, Baxter."

Captain Gringo nodded and said, "Neither do I. Do you want to look under the bed for machineguns?"

He'd been kidding. But the silent partner gravely dropped to his hands and knees to peer under the bed. Then he rose, dusted off his knees, and had a look in the closet. The one who seemed more talkative, said, "I hope you have someone to substantiate your claim you never left the hotel, sir?"

It was Daisy's turn. "I can, Inspector," she said, "but please don't tell the boss-man downstairs that I spent the night with this white gentleman. I told them I was feeling poorly and if they found out where I really spent the night . . ."

The cops smiled, not unkindly, and assured her, "We're not with the vice squad, miss. But for the record, who are you and what connection do you have with this hotel?"

"If you please, sir, I'm Daisy Brooks and I work as a waitress."

"I see. I didn't think I recognized you as one of the, ah, regulars. I don't want to jeopardize your job, Miss Brooks. But you understand we have to make discreet inquiries, and if you've been lying to us . . ."

"Lord of mercy, what would I lie about, sir? You caught me red-faced and bare-behinded, being bad with a white man! What on earth would I be trying to cover up?"

"Hmm, as a matter of fact, you're not covering up as much as you might think. All right, it looks like there must be another tall blond chap who wanders about with machineguns at night. The one we're looking for certainly wasn't seen in the company of a naked colored girl. You did say you weren't planning on staying long, didn't you, uh, Captain?"

"I did, now. I'm just waiting for a boat to take me down the coast."

"Be on it, by the end of this week. Come on, Muldoon. We still have a couple of other leads to check out."

As they left, the one who hadn't said much, growled, "I liked this one best. But you're in charge."

Captain Gringo got up to lock the door behind them. As he turned, he saw Daisy was crying. He got in bed with her and took her in his arms to comfort her, saying, "There, there, it's over and you did swell, Daisy."

"Oh, I felt so ashamed," she sobbed. "They looked at me like I was trash!" Then she stiffened and added, "Oh, Lord of mercy, we're both naked and you're under the sheets with me!"

He said, "I get bashful, too. Don't worry. I'll behave. Let's just wait a minute and make sure they've left before you get dressed and duck out."

"I'm afraid of that, too. The other guests are using the halls now and, oh, Lord, listen to that!"

He cocked his ear, heard the sound of tinkling crockery on a rolling table, and said, "Yeah, someone's having breakfast in bed."

"What'll I *do*? I dare not go out in the hall in my kimono on a guest floor."

"Yeah, we seem to be trapped. *I* dare not go out at *all*! Have you eaten yet? I could send for a big single breakfast and you could hide in the closet while it was delivered, right?"

"I already ate, just before those policemen came into the kitchen asking about you. I can't ask you not to have your breakfast, but, oh, I'm so scared!"

"Hey, no problem. I'll skip my morning coffee. I'm already too wide awake for my own health."

She blushed and added, "I can feel how awake you are," as she moved her hips back a few inches. A few inches wasn't enough. The throbbing tip was still between her naked thighs. He said, "Pay no attention. It has a mind of its own. We can play cards or something to pass the time, if you brought a pack of cards or something."

She laughed and said, "I only brought me, and parts of me have a mind of their own. But I'm trying to make me behave."

"Why? How often does such an opportunity arise?"

"Lord of mercy, your opportunity surely has arisen! But that wasn't why I came here and I wouldn't want you to think I was that kind of gal. I mean, I ain't no goody two-shoes, but..."

He knew exactly what she meant: Dames always seemed to think they had to have an excuse at times like this. He pulled her closer and kissed her to shut her up as he rolled atop her. She tried to say something negative with her tongue in his mouth but her tawny thighs opened in welcome and she thrust her pelvis up to meet his questing shaft. As he entered her she rolled her head wildly from side to side and gasped, "Oh, what are you doing to me?" as she did it back to him—with considerable skill for a waitress. He could tell that while she was no virgin she was really more accustomed to serving ordinary breakfasts. Life was probably lonely in the staff quarters up under the mansard roof. She moved like she hadn't had any for some time and even came before he did.

She came a second time as he ejaculated in her and went limp, caressing her warm breasts. She sighed, "That was lovely, but you must think I'm trash."

He kissed her gently and said, "I think you're an angel of mercy and a good friend, Daisy. Making love to you was just the icing on the cake. I'll never forget what you did for me before."

"I had to. I was so afraid they'd arrest you. Why are they after you, Darling Dick?"

"It's a long story that even bores *me*. How long can you stay here, Honey?"

"You mean you still want me? I thought once you were satisfied you'd feel ashamed and want me to leave."

"You thought dumb. Who on earth would throw a lovely dish like you out of bed, Daisy?"

"That's a long boring story, too," she sighed. "It's why I came here from Jamaica. You see, I worked for this white family and they had a son who said he loved me and . . ."

"Stop right there. I get the picture and it's not a pretty one. Not all men are like that, Daisy."

"White men are. I didn't want to give myself to you, honest. I knew that once you'd had your way with a yellow girl . . ."

"You're talking dumb," he cut in, moving inside her to emphasize his point. But, thanks to his earlier affair in this same bed with the firmer and more athletic Ynez, he was having a problem keeping it up. He enjoyed the contrast of their bodies and he certainly couldn't think of anything that could improve Daisy's throbbing little love maw; but while any normal male can always get it up for single shot action in strange stuff, there were limits, even for him.

But he knew she needed more reassuring than he'd just given her and he was sincerely grateful to her for saving his ass. So he took a leaf from Gaston's book and started kissing her all over, playing with her body like a musical instrument with his mouth and hands in an unselfish attempt to gratify her some more while giving his exhausted tool a rest. Because he wasn't trying to satisfy his own lust, not having enough left to worry about, Daisy found his new tricks delightful indeed.

She rolled her head from side to side, moaning in pleasure, as he kissed his way down over her breasts and belly while skillfully fingering her excited clit. But as he moved his lips down into her lap, teasing her clean pubic hair with his darting tongue, she gasped, "Oh, you don't meant to do *that* to a servant girl of color, do you?"

He thought that sounded pretty dumb, since even if it had been that important to him she was at least three quarters white, fresh as the Daisy she was named after, and hadn't been with another guy for months or more. He parted the pink lips between her tawny thighs and teased the tip of his tongue over her aroused pink clit as he ran two fingers up inside her. It drove her nuts.

She rolled toward him, groping for his own private parts, and started sucking thirstily as he felt her vaginal muscles contracting on his knuckles. Going sixty-nine with a beautiful quadroon in broad daylight inspired him to new heights, too. But he made her come again with his tongue before, not wanting to possibly leave her feeling humiliated when she cooled off, switched ends to finish right.

Daisy clung to him like a warm limpet, with her tawny arms and legs around him as they climaxed once more, together. As they lay exhausted in each other's arms, she sobbed, "Oh, you does love me, after all! I was so afraid you just wanted to use me as your colored play pretty. But I loved you so much I just couldn't help myself."

He kissed her passionately because he couldn't think of a damned thing to say. What was this love shit? Had she been mooning about him up in her little lonely room? What the hell had he started here and, more important, how was he going to end it without hurting a hell of a nice, but not very bright little friend?

• • •

By lunch time Captain Gringo was hungry as a bitch wolf and he'd managed to convince Daisy she should leave before someone found out about her romance with a guest. He went across the hall to Gaston's room so they could eat together and make some serious plans for the very near future.

Gaston, alone and dressed, too, for a change, listened soberly as Captain Gringo brought him up to date while they ate. Then Gaston said, "*Parbleu* and *damn!* Can't I leave you alone five minutes without you falling in love, you oversexed moose! You really ought to just pay for it, like your elders. It saves so much time in the morning!"

Captain Gringo grinned sheepishly and said, "I didn't fall in love with anybody. It was her idea."

"No matter. The point is that now you have yourself set up for a most *fatigue* bedroom farce with two passionate wenches dashing in and out of your door at any moment! I thought we were trying not to attract attention here, my old and sex crazed! Has that wild Basque girl tried to contact you?"

"Not so far, and I don't mind telling you I was wondering what I'd say if the phone rang while I was in bed with Daisy. I told Daisy not to come back uninvited. She cried a lot, but I think she understands that a guy on the run has to be careful. She shouldn't feel rejected, this time, when I have to flee for my life. I laid it on a little about having to renounce going home with her to meet her mother because she was too nice a girl to be mixed up with a knockaround bum with a price on his head."

"*Merde alors,* you told her the simple truth. What about Ynez?"

"Same deal. She was probably scared out of a year's

growth last night and by now she may have second thoughts about her private war with El Cazador."

"True, a machinegun burst in the face tends to convince one of the other side's sincerity. But she has *money,* Dick."

"Not enough to matter. This hotel is turning out to be a worthless, as well as expensive hideout. So, since anyone who's really looking for us seems to know we're here, we may as well save on the rent."

"*Oui,* eliminating both romantic entanglements, and possibly surprising El Cazador as well. If we leave during La Siesta, in a few minutes, now, trailing us through the streets should be difficult, non?"

"Yeah, but we'll wait until anyone staked out will be in some shade or other to keep their brains from frying."

"Ah, *oui,* with rooftop snipers taking a break we can duck out the back way and . . ."

"Wrong. Guys ducking out the back way are going some place sneaky. It's not that tough to have all exits covered. Our bet is to stroll out the front entrance, telling anyone who asks that we'll be back in a little while. I've been looking over the waterfront from my own room. There's no place between here and the quay to set up an ambush without some passing constable noticing enough to ask questions."

"*Eh bein,* and then what do we do, start swimming?"

"No. We're meeting a guy I phoned a while ago. Padre Junipero says he can't come personally, but he's sending a sexton from the church to meet us at that café down the quay with the machinegun and spare ammo, wrapped in a tarp, of course."

Gaston frowned and said, "You certainly are good at making friends. But that *café* seems an odd place to meet anyone, after the excitement we had there the last time, non?"

"That's why I told Padre Junipero to deliver the guns

there. It's called back-tracking when a fox does it. The café will be open during la siesta. The waiter shouldn't recognize us, shaved and wearing respectable clothes. El Cazador won't expect us to be there, of all places."

"Perhaps. But what if he hunts foxes as well as people?"

"Tough shit. You saw the other day that there's no cover around the café. So he'll have to fight us in the open, and I sure am looking forward to that!"

Gaston finished his coffee, put down the cup, and said, "I can't think of anything better. *Eh bien,* we go to the café, get the machinegun, and then what? I have seen you handle a machinegun, but a Maxim is a heavy load for romping along the beach with, non?"

"Yeah, we have to have transportation, too. I said I've been watching out the front window. There's only one vessel tied up near enough to matter. There's not another vessel moored anywhere near it. The crew seemed to have come ashore. There's one clown standing watch in the cockpit, but that's *his* problem."

"Sacre bleu! You intend to commit piracy?"

"Why not? We've committed everything else. It's a fore and aft schooner with an auxiliary engine—oil fired, from the smoke. Her sails are reefed, so we don't have to bother about them. We'll just swipe her and head up the coast, see?"

"No, I don't see! It sounds wild as the devil, even for you! But what is this *up* the coast, my old and bucaneering? Don't you mean *down* the coast?"

"No. Too many people are expecting us to head back for Costa Rica. So we'll snatch ourselves a schooner and head north."

"Toward Mexico and El Cazador's headquarters?"

"Why not? The bastard's looking for us, isn't he? I'm tired of running when there's no place we can go that he can't follow. So let's just drop in on the prick with a machinegun and see what the hell he aims to do about it!"

Gaston made the sign of the cross and said, "*Mon Dieu,* he means it! Who does that schooner belong to, Dick?"

"How the hell should I know? I've never seen it before. The point is that it's *there,* with only one or two guys guarding it, so it's ours if we want it, and I want it."

"I don't wish to quibble about property rights, my adorable child, but for God's sake, it's broad daylight outside!"

"So what? People *expect* you to pirate a schooner when it's *dark*!"

The sexton from the church had delivered the wrapped-up Maxim and ammo box in a donkey cart. As Captain Gringo lugged it down the quay on his shoulder he could see why: it was heavy as hell in the shimmering noon-day heat. Gaston carried the ammo box, which only looked like a tin box from any distance, and there was nobody else dumb enough to be out on the open quay at this hour.

Gaston was bitching again as they approached the schooner tied up alone just ahead. He said, "Dick, this is crazy! Look at all those windows to our right. The whole town will be watching as we try to steam that yacht out of the harbor!"

"No they won't—just the ones looking out the windows. I watched the schooner come in yesterday, and *I* didn't think about calling the cops. Why should anyone else? I didn't notice any pilot boat bothering with a shallow draft schooner when they came in. The harbor master is probably holed up somewhere with a gin and tonic, not expecting anyone to leave."

"But what if that vessel's owners are watching from

one of those windows you seem to feel so confident about, hein?"

"They'll probably get excited as hell. But why should anybody be sitting in a window staring at a tub they just got off? And what can they do to stop us if they are? By the time they can call the law, we'll be heading out to sea and there's nothing faster moored in the harbor right now. Relax, Gaston. Have I ever gotten you killed yet?"

"There is always a first time. I don't see anyone on deck ahead."

"I do. He's sitting under that awning over the cockpit hatch. There's a faint smudge of smoke from that foreward funnel, too. We're in luck. They've kept the steam up. So we won't have to hang around while we build pressure in the boiler. As soon as we're aboard, you man the helm while I check below decks, start the engine, and pop back up to cast off. I want the screw turning at full rev before we let go the hausers, see?"

"*Merde alors,* you are putting the cart before the horse. We have to capture the damned schooner first, Dick!"

"Yeah, cover me. We're almost to the gangplank."

Gaston muttered darkly under his breath as Captain Gringo strode up the gangplank like he owned the schooner. The crewman hunkered in the shade didn't think he did, got up and moved forward, asking, "What are you doing aboard this vessel, señor?"

Captain Gringo pointed the .38 in his free hand at him and said, "Don't ask foolish questions. Are you alone on board? I get surly when people tell me fibs."

The crewman blanched and said, "*Por favor,* señor, I am only a watchman!"

"I didn't ask you who you were. I don't give a *fuck* who you are. Is there anyone else aboard?"

"No, señor, everyone else is ashore. I am not a regular member of the crew. I was hired from the beach for to guard the gangplank. You are making the joke about being pirates, no?"

"Move aft and keep this gun in my hand in mind. We'll put you ashore out around the narrows if you behave yourself. Get cute and we won't. Are you behind me, Gaston?"

"*Oui.* I must have lost my mind."

"Okay, take this guy back to the cockpit and sit on him while you man the helm. I'm going below."

He made room for Gaston to pass him on the narrow deck. He placed the wrapped Maxim atop the cabin for now and followed them as far back as a side hatch in the cabin wall. He slid it open and dropped down into the cabin, squinting in the sudden gloom. As his eyes adjusted he saw he was in the main salon. It was empty. Moving forward he found the engine room ahead of the galley, went down a short ladder and checked out the boiler. As he'd hoped, it was steam fired and the gauges said the pressure was up. He looked for the throttle, saw the one in the engine room was pantographed to work in unison with another probably up near the helm. He opened the throttle and felt the duckboards vibrating under his boots as the screw started turning over. That was enough for the engine room. He climbed out to see what else they had aboard.

Ahead of the engine room on the main deck he found luxuriously appointed but empty staterooms with private heads. A crew's compartment and head were up in the bows, with the chain locker. He moved aft again, found a hatchway leading down to the hold, and opened it to see what sort of goodies they were carrying below the waterline. It was dark as hell. He struck a match, then quickly shook it out as he heard a moan!

He moved out of the shaft of overhead light from the hatch as he growled, "Okay, who and where are you!"

He was answered with an urgent muffled groan. He

moved toward it, gingerly, squeezing between crates and barrels until he could make out a dim form on the bilge boards. Whoever it was was making the odd noises. So he struck another light and muttered, "What the hell?"

It was Ynez. She lay with hands and ankles locked in hand cuffs, wearing nothing but her black silk teddy, silk stockings, and a strip of tape across her mouth. Dropping to his knees at her side, he said, "Sorry, this is going to sting" and yanked the tape away in one quick jerk. Ynez gasped, "Oh, my God, I'm so glad you found me, Darling! How did you know I was here?"

"Lucky guess," he answered. "We'll worry about those cuffs later. "We've got to get out of here!"

He picked her up and carried her up from the hold as she explained, "They grabbed me as I was on my way to your hotel about four hours ago! Oh, Dick, I thought I'd never see you again!"

He repressed a smile as he considered what she'd have found him doing at the hotel had she made it. He asked, "Does this tub belong to who I think it does, Doll?" and she replied, "It must be El Cazador's. But I did not see him when they brought me here."

He carried her into the main salon, placed her on a couch, and instructed, "Don't go 'way. I'll have Gaston pick those locks as soon as he has a little free time."

She asked him what he was up to as he was leaving, but he was in too big a hurry to answer. He rejoined Gaston in the cockpit. The so-called watchman was within reach, so Captain Gringo pistol whipped him to the deck, kicked him to make sure he was out, and growled, "I told him not to fib. They had Ynez chained up in the hold. This seems to be our lucky day. We're stealing El Cazador's private yacht! Hang on to the wheel while I cast off!"

Captain Gringo ran forward, hauled in the gangplank, and cast off the hausers. The schooner was moving by the time he made it back to Gaston, picking up the Maxim on the way.

Gaston set a course for the open sea as Captain Gringo scanned the shore for anybody wanting to make anything out of it. The patchwork of stucco, tile, and corrugated iron was doing a silent shimmy dance in the vertical rays of the tropical sun. But he could make out some dots running along the quay from the north. Nobody ran like that in la siesta hour unless they were excited about something. Yeah, one of them was shaking his fist out across the water at them. He waved bye-bye and told Gaston, "We just made it. Can you get any more revolutions out of that screw?"

"*Mais non,* you can see the throttle is at full speed. Le petite engine was never designed with steaming in mind, Dick. If you would glance aloft you would see this was a sailing vessel with just enough auxiliary power to navigate sedately when the trades are not blowing, which is seldom."

Captain Gringo saw they were out of gunshot range from the shore, now, and said, "Oh well, those guys don't seem to be doing anything but running up and down sort of confused. Can you pick the locks of regulation hand cuffs?"

"Can a hen lay eggs?"

"That's what I thought. I'll take the helm while you get Ynez out of those cuffs. Don't screw her unless she asks you to, and see if you can find her clothes before you bring her out on deck. We've got enough to worry about without a sunburned kidnap victim on our hands."

Gaston traded places with him and went below as Captain Gringo swung the bow a bit to the north and steamed toward the harbor narrows. The owners of the tub might be afraid to run to the Brits and yell Pirate since they knew a police launch would find a lady they'd kidnapped aboard. On the other hand, they might be that dumb, and the sooner he swung the yacht around that point of land to the north and out of sight the better.

The black hull was shallow draft and he knew the channel markers were meant for deep draft freighters. He looked back over his shoulder. The crew members were heading inland away from the waterfront, so they were going some damned place to tell somebody. The schooner had overcome inertia and was moving as fast as its engine told it to, but it wasn't moving all that fast. He figured they were making six knots. He also figured there had to be a better way. But even if Ynez knew something about sailing, they were too short-handed to hoist the brown canvas. Getting the sails up wasn't the problem. Tacking athwart the trades wasn't the problem. Reefing the sails in a sudden squall was the problem. You had to think ahead in the hurricane season.

He was thinking about how much bunker oil they had when Gaston and Ynez rejoined him in the cockpit. The girl was wearing a man's khaki shirt a size too big for her, so she was sort of shapeless above the tops of her long black stockings. From there down she was all girl. She was in her stocking feet. Now that he had a better look at her in the sunlight, he saw they'd cut off her long black hair, too. Gaston said, "We could not find what they did with her clothes and shoes," and Ynez sobbed, "They took all my money, too! I had borrowed more, to see if I could talk you into helping me and . . ."

"Never mind," Captain Gringo cut in, reaching one hand out to pat the tarp covered machinegun as he added, "Old El Cazador keeps giving us convincing arguments. We've got to stomp him before he really hurts somebody. I'm sorry about your hair. I know Latin types have a thing about giving haircuts to pretty girls. Uh, is that all they did, Ynez?"

She sat down beside him, grimaced, and replied, "I wasn't raped, if that's what you mean."

"That's what I mean. It looks like El Cazador recruits among his own kind. Most mariposas are like the rest of us when it comes to cruelty. But there's nothing nastier than a bitchy fag."

Ynez ran her fingers experimentally through her shorter but not really disastrous new hairdo as she mused, "I never took Roderico Montalban for one of those. I told you I met his wife, before he turned on us."

"We met her, too. Montalban's what we call a closet queen in the States. Or maybe he's just a capon. There's definitely something wrong with his glands."

Gaston held out a sheaf of penciled papers and said, "He writes *très* mysterious, too. I found these notes along with one of those new Marconi sets in what must be the master state room. I took the liberty of tearing them from the pad as Señora Ynez was rummaging in his locker for something to wear. What language would you say this was, Dick?"

Captain Gringo took a sheet and read, "TEO: RAOTYOAILN CSOHNRSDTLAUBEUALOAIRNY, BEEALTIOZIE..." Before he gave up and asked Ynez to tell him if it was Basque. She said it wasn't. He said, "Looks like some sort of code, then. We'll worry about it later. Oboy, Gaston, you'd better take the wheel. Ynez, go back below and put your fingers in your ears. We'll wake you when it's over."

"What do you mean, Dick?" the Basque girl gasped. "What is wrong?" and as he changed places with Gaston and whipped the tarp off the Maxim he pointed ashore at the spot they were approaching to say, "Alexander Graham Bell. It used to be a lot easier to vanish from human ken before that son-of-a-bitch invented the telephone!"

Gaston said, "I see them, Dick. I think you're right. That shore party does not look like they are looking for a place to have a picnic. We'd better swing wide, out of rifle range, unless those are brooms they are carrying, hein?"

"No. Steady as she goes. This Maxim can't carry any farther than a rifle round. Damn it, Ynez, move your sweet fanny!"

She moved it very nicely indeed as she ducked under the low overhang of the hatchway and dropped down into the main salon. As Captain Gringo fed one end of the ammo belt into the action and cocked the Maxim, the deck watch he'd cold cocked sat up, rubbing his head and muttering in confusion. Captain Gringo snapped, "Stay where you are unless you want to go swimming." But the groggy crewman put a hand on the gunwhale and pulled himself to his unsteady feet just as a rifle squibbed from the trees ashore on the point. A hot lead slug hit the erstwhile deck watch in the chest with an audible thunk. So Captain Gringo ignored the results as he dropped to his knees, braced the Maxim over the edge of the cockpit, and opened up. He hosed a traverse of machinegun fire at knee level, just below the white blossoms of rifle smoke blossoming along the shore against the spinach green backdrop. Then he swept the hot muzzle of the Maxim back the other way to dust off the ones he'd dropped with a lower elevation. He was traversing the Maxim a third time when it choked on the end of the belt and fell silent. But what the hell, they were passing the point and nobody was firing at them now.

Steaming up the mosquito coast at a crawl in broad daylight after sounding off with a machinegun within earshot of a major colonial seaport could be dangerous to one's health. So as soon as they were well clear of Belize and saw no sign of anyone else on land or sea, Captain

Gringo steered for shore—dead slow—and found an inlet in the swampy mangrove flats to hole up and lay low while they considered their next moves.

Ynez explored the galley and discovered there was plenty of canned food and said she loved to cook. So they let her as they remained on watch in the cockpit with a view out to sea between the mangroves. There wasn't much they could do about the bloodstains, but of course they'd tossed the dead crew member overboard after finding nothing interesting in his pockets.

Captain Gringo was studying the mysterious message penciled on the note paper from the master state room as Gaston bitched about steaming at night with an engine only meant for getting about harbors. Captain Gringo ignored him. They'd already agreed they'd be in even more trouble if a gunboat spotted them in broad daylight. He took a pencil stub from his shirt pocket and started experimenting with the coded letters as he asked Gaston if the marconi set was a two-way. Gaston said, "*Mais non,* it is only a crystal receiver. Why?"

"Hardly anybody has wireless telegraphs yet. The invention is brand new with a lot of bugs to work out. But anybody can take down dots and dashes, and crystal sets are easy to find and easy to work. It looks like our great white hunter isn't in communication by short wave with anybody in particular. He likes to listen in on *other* people's conversations."

"Ahah, then these notes were transcribed from an intercepted message from . . . whom?"

"Probably someone official. The few ships equipped with marconi sets send their S.O.S.'s in the clear. Let's see, you wouldn't waste time with a complicated code when it was a hundred-to-one nobody would intercept it in the first place. They taught us the easy ciphers at West Point, when we could have used more info on Apache tactics. It's got to be Spanish, English, or maybe

French, in this neck of the woods. I'll cross out every other letter for openers. That's the easy cipher lots of guys use and, hey, it works! Look what I've done!"

Gaston took the first sheet and read, "TEO: RAOT-YOAILN CSOHNRSDTLAUBEUALOAIRNY, BE-EALTIOZIE" with every other letter crossed out to read, "TO ROYAL CONSTABULARY, BELIZE." He laughed and said, "You are a genius! Who do you think sent this—Greystoke?"

"No, British Intelligence could do better than this. It's probably a diplomatic code used by the British Foreign Office. Lots of dim-witted guys with the right old-school ties, take jobs where they can get 'em."

He rapidly crossed out other letters, now that he'd broken the cipher, and laughed aloud. Gaston asked what was so funny. Captain Gringo said, "This explains why El Cazador was so shy about shooting it out with us in Belize, and why he was so coy about personal appearances. The authorities in British East Africa have a *warrant* out on the bastard! It seems they've made peace with the tribesmen they were huffing and puffing at. So now it turns out El Cazador was even a bigger bastard than they thought. They knew he'd gunned more natives than the situation really called for, so they asked him to go play someplace else. But it turns out he and some Arabs working with him took some of the quarry alive and sold them as slaves to Zanzibar traders. I guess he wanted to break even on expenses."

"Slaving is illegal in the British colonies, non?"

"Yeah, you're allowed to *shoot* darkies for Queen Vickie, but she frowns on needlessly confusing the servant problem. Anyhow, El Cazador is now *persona non grata* in all British colonies. Mexico still likes him and has no extradition treaty with Great Britain, but the Brits mean to *hang* El Cazador the next time they see him!"

"*Sacre bleu!* Wasn't he taking a hell of a chance in following us to Belize, then?"

"Hell, don't you *get* it? He never showed his face in Belize. He just sent his goons to shake us up so we'd run somewhere he *could* have a personal crack at us! Jesus, I've heard of monomaniacs, but this guy takes the cake! El Tigre and the others had orders not to mar his trophies. That's what all the fucking around was about, see?"

"*Mais non,* I do not see at all. Last night they tried to mar you indeed with that machinegun, and as we were leaving, those were not cream puffs they were casting our way, remember?"

"So guys get excited. Like I said, that ambush near Ynez's wasn't meant for me. They were after her because she was running all around trying to hire some guns to go after the turd, and apparently he doesn't consider women important enough to hunt down personally. Maybe he thinks it would hurt his machismo image to gun women. He was willing to settle for driving his wife to suicide, remember? As for the guys who just shot it out with us, they were probably nervous about being stranded in a strange port and didn't wait for orders from the boss. He's probably up the coast a ways and, hold it, that's what the radio is about. Sure, he was sending his commands by short wave. The intercepted British message was just for practice. He already knew they were mad at him or he wouldn't be playing it so safe, see?"

Gaston grimaced and said, "I find it *très fatigue* to strain my jolly brain trying to outguess a maniac. El Cazador's logic eludes me. So does yours. You say you think he is a homosexual, yet he worries about his image as a macho-man?"

Captain Gringo fished out a smoke and lit it as he thought about that. Then he nodded and said, "Sure. He has to. El Presidente Diaz and his brutal rurales are sons-of-bitches, but they're hairy chested sons-of-bitches. Hispanics take mariposas more seriously than we do and you can get twenty years in some states for sodomy. The inquisition used to burn homosexuals at the stake. Calling a man a queer is more serious than calling him a mother-fucker in Spanish-speaking countries. So whatever our spoiled Basque brat does with his pecker, he doesn't let his Mexican amigos *know* about it! He married Morgana before coming back to Mexico because he knew an English girl would be less apt to gossip about his prowess in bed with the neighbors than a native girl would. He probably had some gossip, already, to worry about in Quintana Roo. His rough hewn pals might have thought it was fun to hunt peasants instead of pheasants, but they must have commented from time to time about his lack of interest in rape and other healthy rurale sports. But screw his unusual love life. I'm more worried about his other hobbies. He's not out to make love to either of us. He wants to make rugs out of us!"

"I hope you are speaking metaphorically, Dick. I still find it a bit unsettling to one's digestion when I remember those shrunken heads our jolly Jivaro hosts had hanging in the dining room that time."

As if the mention of upset digestion had been her cue, Ynez came out on deck with a tray of Moors and Christians, saying, "I hope you two won't mind that the beans are from a can. There's proper rice in the galley, but I've never made this with canned beans before."

They took their tin plates and dug in. The Moors and Christians were no better nor worse than they'd eaten everywhere else in Latin America. The Moors were the beans and the Christians of course were the grains of rice. It was simple hearty fare that stuck to the ribs and Captain Gringo had a good appetite from the sea air. So he told her they were swell and Gaston laid it on more than the simple repast really called for. Captain

Gringo wondered if Gaston had the hots for his girl. There was nothing he could do about it if Ynez said yes. He knew she didn't say *no* with any real conviction and what the hell, it would simplify things. Ynez had more than enough to offer any one man and he had to keep his strength up. To let them work it out, if they were going to, and because it really was a bother to have a machinegun and no ammo, he finished his plate and said he was going exploring. Ynez fucked up Gaston's sex life by coming with him as Gaston stood watch.

His earlier tour of the vessel had been hurried and he'd only been looking for moving targets. This time he opened drawers and doors as he prowled the foreward state rooms. They found the marconi set where it was supposed to be, in what had to be the master state room. He saw the bed was made up, but the covers were dented as if someone had been laying on them since the last real overhaul. It figured whoever listened to the wireless had to sit somewhere. A neat high-powered rifle with a scope sight was mounted on the mahogany bulkhead above the built-in bed. As he took it down, Ynez said El Cazador had similar guns on every wall at his plantation house to the north. He drew the bolt and muttered, "Nuts, these express rounds won't fit the Maxim. But they couldn't have only sent along one lousy box of machinegun ammo." He stepped over to a built-in closet and opened it.

Ynez screamed.

He didn't blame her. A human head was staring at them from the shelf above the coat hangers, stuffed or preserved some other way.

As Ynez sank to the bed and covered her face with her hands, he swallowed the green taste in his stomach and slid the door shut, saying, "Some buys collect stamps, some guys are just crazy. Didn't you notice that when you were digging out that shirt, Doll?"

"I opened the other closet, thank God! Who *was* that, Dick?"

"Beats me. Looks like he was an Hispanic, when he was alive. Oh, I see the one you mean."

He opened the other closet. It, too, had mostly hunting togs hanging in it. Fortunately nothing worse. He found some mosquito boots on the floor under the hanging clothes and kicked a pair out, saying, "Try these on for size, Doll. You'll get splinters running around in your stocking feet."

But Ynez shook her cropped head and said, "No, I couldn't. How could I wear the boots of such a monster?" Then she gasped and added, "Oh, I have one of his shirts on!" and proceeded to pull it off, popping the buttons. He liked what he saw as she stood up after tossing it aside. But it wasn't practical deck gear. He said, "Look, let's go back up to the crew's quarters and see if we can find you a sailor suit."

She followed, but protested, "How can I be sure I won't be putting on *another* monster's clothing, Darling?"

"You can't be *sure*, but it's an educated guess nobody else could be as monstrous as El Cazador. Tell yourself the duds belong to a simple sailor lad who just works for the bastard. It could be true."

They got to the crew's quarters where he found a sea bag that looked clean. He spilled out the contents on a bunk and said, "Good. This stuff just came back from the laundry. Here's a striped jersey and a pair of dungarees. Put them on while I look for some rope-soled sandals."

He dropped to one knee to peer under the bunks as Ynez sat on another bunk and started rolling down her silk stockings. That seemed reasonable. But then she started taking off her teddy. He hauled a pair of sandals out from under another bunk and placed them by her bare feet, as her nude breasts came into view. Grinning he said, "I guess you don't need underwear unless you split the dungarees. But for God's sake put them on pronto. You're giving me a hard-on."

Ynez smiled, leaned back with her feet on the decking and her thighs spread as she said, "Why don't we do something about it, then?"

He started to say no, but then wondered why the hell he'd want to say a silly thing like that. Gaston was on watch and there was nobody else on board to disturb them.

He grinned, knelt between her inviting thighs, and dropped his pants as he said, "Let's make it a quicky, though. We still have to find that ammo and Gaston will wonder what's taking us so long."

But of course, once he was in her, it didn't seem so important that they had other things to do. They were stuck in this cove until sunset and, as Ynez pointed out, they could hardly do this and sail the vessel at the same time. So he took off his shirt as well, and they wound up doing it right on the bunk together. He'd forgotten how yummy Ynez was, thanks to his morning adventure with the softer, darker Daisy. He propped himself up on locked elbows to enjoy the new view as Ynez moaned, "Oh, you are so virile! I feared you would not be able to make love to me again so soon, after all we did together last night!"

He'd been afraid of that, too. Closing his eyes and picturing Daisy in the same position then opening them for a nice surprise helped a lot. They came the old-fashioned way, did it again dog-style, and then Ynez begged for mercy, saying, "Not again, Dear. Save some for later. I'm not used to so much sex since my husband was murdered." But then, as he started to take it out, she arched her spine and sighed, "Wait, come to think of it, I wasn't getting it like this *before* poor Carlos was taken from me. I think I can stand one more time after all."

He wasn't sure he could, but the view was inspired and

they managed a long shuddering mutual orgasm as they collapsed across the rumpled mattress. Then he said, "Lay here and rest a while, Doll. I've got things to do."

He rolled off, hauled on his things, and left her cooing to herself as he went down into the hold. This time he found a lamp screwed to a bulkhead and lit it for a better view. The small hold was laden mostly with ships stores, of course. But he grinned in delight as he found a crate marked, "Fabrique National," and opened it to see roll on roll of belted Maxim ammo. The canvas would stay drier down here in the hold if it rained so he only took out a couple of belts for now.

He found Ynez dressed like a stacked common seaman and they went back up to rejoin Gaston. Captain Gringo dropped the ammo belts by the machinegun braced against the rail and said, "We're back in business. Anything interesting happen while we were below?"

"Not on deck," Gaston said dryly, with a pointed but admiring glance at the way Ynez filled out her striped jersey and too-tight white dungarees. The Basque girl blushed and said something about seeing to the dishes as she picked up the used plates on the tray and went below for the moment. Gaston chuckled and remarked, "They always think others can tell. That's how others can always tell."

Captain Gringo smiled sheepishly and said, "Guilty, Your Honor. It's a little early for me to try and fix you up. But if we're going to have her along any length of time . . ."

"Forget it," Gaston cut in, adding, "I'd love some of that, but one must be *practique* as well as lustful. That one is ga-ga for you, Dick. If you suggested sharing the wealth it would only upset her."

"I'm glad you see it that way. I'd rather share tobacco any day. Now that it's settled who she sleeps with, we have to think of a nice way to get rid of her."

"*Parbleu,* is the honeymoon over so soon?"

"No, but she'll probably start bitching about why I can't get a regular job by the time we make it to Quintana Roo. They all do. That's not the reason we have to put her ashore somewhere, though. It's slowly dawning on me that the guy we're after is a frothing-at-the-mouth dangerous lunatic. He's already tried to kill her, snatch her, and for all I know, have her stuffed. I found a trophy head in his closet—suitable to be mounted on a wall. We can't afford to take Ynez with us all the way."

"*Merde alors,* we can't afford to take *us* all the way! What if we were to beach this schooner somewhere just up the coast and forget the whole distressing business, hein? We know El Cazador is afraid to show his face in British Honduras."

"Yeah, but so am I. The cops at the hotel told me they didn't want to see me in the colony after this weekend. I think they meant it. Great Britain only wants El Cazador for slaving. Have you forgotten I'm wanted for everything but chicken pox? Besides, abandoning this tub would put us right back where we started. I found it tedious as hell. El Cazador has a mad desire to mount our heads in his trophy room no matter where we go, so let's go shoot the mother-fucker and get it over with!"

Gaston smiled crookedly and replied, "Crudely put, but *practique. Eh bièn,* we shall need help, if only to man this vessel properly before we run out of fuel as we creep up the coast like a crippled duck. After dark, let us make for San Pedro, on Ambergris Cay, non?"

"Maybe. Run Ambergris Cay by me again. I've never heard about it."

"Ah, I sometimes forget how new to the game you are. Ambergris Cay is an island off to the north-east. It is British owned, and in the buccaneer era San Pedro was a pirate port. Since then it has subsided to merely a *très* disreputable place inhabited by various rogues of all nationalities. The royal governor back in Belize doubtless has it on his map, but no important British officials have visited the place in living memory. There is nothing there worth taxing. The natives live by fishing, beach combing, and so forth. San Pedro is a truly dreadful little port. Naturally, any old comrades I might meet there should be *très* anxious to sign on as pirates or whatever we tell them this is all about."

"Sounds okay. But what makes you think you'll run into anyone you know on Ambergris Cay? Like I said, I never heard of the place."

"Ah, that is why rogues on the run hide out there. As to them being rogues I might know, I know *most* of the rogues in Latin America. Trust me, even if we can't find a crew, a lady rogue I know there runs a *très* unusual house of joy."

Captain Gringo laughed, "That's not a problem for me right now. I'm trying to get rid of some joy. Do you think we could ditch Ynez in San Pedro?"

"*Oui,* but it would be a dirty trick to play on a respectable white woman. The only way off the cay is via an occasional mail boat or smuggler's craft, and she might find the natives more friendly than she bargained for."

"I get the picture. Okay, say we recruit a few hard cases to help us, where's the next best place to drop her off?"

"Corozal?"

"Nuts to Corozal. That's where El Cazador came in. Besides, there's a harbor patrol there and we don't know what those guys we stole this schooner from might have told the colonial authorities."

"True. They might have fibbed about us, and one could be sticky about ships' papers and so forth. Let me see. They took her money and we can only spare a few bills, since we only have a few bills between us. If we put into Xcalak, on the Mexican side of the line . . . *oui,*

Xcalak is little more than an Indian fishing village. But there is a Catholic mission at Xcalak. It's on a peninsula and out of the way, even for a lowland jungle port. The mission will shelter her until she can send home for passage. That is if she will agree to it, of course."

"We'll worry about that when the time comes to say adios. Meanwhile we still have to worry about just where in hell we're going after we lighten the load. I forgot to ask her what this tub's home port might be."

"We wish to sail into El Cazador's home port, Dick?"

"We don't wish to, but the last I heard, it was hard to catch a street car in the Mexican lowland jungles. Ynez and her late husband had the plantation next door to El Cazador's. So naturally she'll know where he loads his produce for shipping and naturally he'd use the same port to sail this tub out of. We'll sail it in, load up on ammo, and hike the rest of the way, see?"

Ynez came back out on deck, having washed the dishes and recovered her poise. "We were just talking about Quintana Roo, Honey," Captain Gringo said. "I forgot to ask you the nearest port to where we're going."

She sat down and answered, "Oh, that's easy: it's a little town called Xcalak. That's where Carlos and I disembarked from Spain, and of course Roderico Montalban was there first."

Then she noted the thoughtful look the two soldiers of fortune exchanged and added, "Did I say something wrong? You both seem a little upset."

They waited until after dark before they made the run for Ambergris Cay. Calling it a run was an overstatement. It was less than fifty sea miles to Ambergris Cay but it took them most of the night and almost all their bunker oil to make it on auxiliary power alone.

The hours at sea weren't completely wasted. Gaston manned the helm as Captain Gringo spent most of the time below decks, checking out the engine gauges, getting to know the vessel better, and calming down Ynez with an occasional kiss or more, as she followed him around like a love-sick pup. She said she wanted to go all the way with him. He was willing to lay her, but he said it was too dangerous for her to go all the way to El Cazador's home port. He explained, "After we pick up a crew and some more fuel at Amberbris Cay we'll put you ashore on the safe side of Chetumal Bay. We'll whip into a fishing village I know within a buggy ride of Corozal. Meanwhile I'll leave you with enough to cat on."

"But I don't want to be left behind, Darling. Don't you love me?"

"Hey, if I were mad at you I wouldn't worry about risking a brush with the British Coast patrols to leave you on a safe shore! Not that anywhere along this coast is really safe with El Cazador running around without a leash. He's already tried to kill you as well as me, Ynez. Be sensible."

"I don't want to be sensible! I want to go on sleeping with you. You'll need me to guide you to the Montalban plantation, no?"

He frowned and said, "Good question," as he headed for the chart case in the main salon with Ynez following. He rummaged through the yacht's large-scale coastal navigation charts until he found the one he was after. He spread it on the fold-down table and said, "Okay, here's the blowup of Chetumal Bay and, Jesus, Mexico's Xcalak Point comes down from the north to almost touch Ambergris Cay! You could damned near swim from the British Cay to El Cazador's backyard. I make that channel only a couple of miles across."

"It's full of sharks. I've never been on Ambergris Cay, but I know the peninsula all too well."

"Good," said Captain Gringo, handing her a pencil as he added, "I want you to pinpoint the location of El Cazador's home plate. As you see, this map has the towns and main roads on it, but makes no mention of private property lines."

Ynez leaned over the map table, concentrated, and drew a pencil line from the fishing village of Xcalak north, across blank paper that she said was lowland jungle and mangrove swamp. She made two little circles and said, "Here's my stolen plantation. The one to the west is Roderico Montalban's. If he hasn't torn it down by now, my old house is simply wooden with a corrugated metal roof and so forth. El Cazador prefers the baronial style. His place, about three of your Anglo miles from mine, is built like a fortress with walls of coral block and corner towers."

"You mean his casa is a castle?"

"Well, a small one. I said he took himself seriously. He even has a coat of arms over the gate. You're going to need help getting in, Dick. I know many people in the neighborhood and, unlike El Cazador, my late husband and I got along well with local peasantry."

"I'm sure you did. But if the locals weren't scared skinny of the rich bastard they'd have burned him out by now. It's going to have to be an outside job, with professionals hitting that stronghold after I scout and see if the prick is home. I'd hate to smoke up all that masonry only to find he was out to lunch."

Captain Gringo took the pencil from Ynez and drew some lines of his own as he mused, "Hmm, there's a salt water creek here, running inland almost to his back door. He has to have informants in the fishing village. Our best bet would be to avoid putting in at Xcalak itself. If we steamed up this channel to within a mile or so of his castle... what's this line you drew from the town, a wagon trace?"

"No, it's a narrow gauge railway. It runs on beyond my place and his, but I don't know to where or how far, since we only used it to transport our produce to the port from our plantation."

"Gotcha, what did you guys and El Cazador grow, Ynez?"

She shrugged and answered, "We intended to ship coffee once our trees matured. El Cazador let us clear the land and put in the trees before he killed my husband and seized our plantation."

"Sweet guy. Is he in the coffee business, too?"

"No, and my late husband was wondering about that. Roderico Montalban was rather evasive about just what he might or might not be growing on his plantation. He must grow something on his own land, but we never found out just what it was."

"Hmm, maybe he just thinks of it as his hunting preserve. The hell with it. We're not going there to harvest his crops. We have to settle his hash."

He put the charts away. Ynez said she wanted to make love some more, but he wanted to arrive at Ambergris Cay with enough strength to matter. He told her they could tear off some more ass crossing the bay to drop her off near the borderline. She stamped her foot, said she didn't want to wait that long, and demanded, "What will become of me if you and Gaston fail to get El Cazador?"

"You'll have to cable home for passage money back to Spain," he said. "If he can take us out, forget your plantation, he's nobody to mess with!"

That seemed to upset her, so naturally he had to comfort her and of course they wound up together on a bunk they hadn't tried yet, though they'd run out of new positions. He left her screwed-drowsy under a sheet as he dressed and went topside to spell Gaston at the wheel. He told Gaston he could go below and catch forty, but

Gaston said he was expecting old Ambergris Cay to rise with the sun on the eastern horizon and the sky was already pearling conch shell pink to the east. So Gaston got to his feet to stomp his feet awake and rub his palms back to life against his pants as Captain Gringo manned the helm and enjoyed the dentist drill vibrations of the wheel spokes for a time. He grimaced and said, "The screw must have a badly bent blade. We're not getting enough R.P.M.s for balanced drive to twang like that."

"*Merde alors,* tell me something I haven't been trying to steer for hours. Speaking of twanging, where's your lady love at the moment, Dick?"

"Don't talk dirty. She's kipped out, regaining her strength to attack me again. Are you sure we can't leave her in San Pedro? Running her all the way back across the bay before we hit El Cazador could cost us almost an extra day."

"I didn't know we were in such a hurry. *Eh bein,* I shall ask when we arrive, but don't bank on it, Dick. As I said, San Pedro is one *très* rough port. And, speaking of the devil, regard those lights winking at us along the horizon line!"

As Captain Gringo did, he noticed their bow was pointing to the south of the harbor lights ahead, so he swung two points north and gazed at the single strand necklace of firefly tails. "I'm surprised to find so many lights on at this hour."

Gaston shrugged and said, "They haven't all gone to bed at the same time since Morgan buried a treasure somewhere along the beach and told them to watch it for him. The rogues of Ambergris Cay sleep only in shifts, with a good friend keeping an eye on their shoes. The town, such as it is, is wide open day and night."

As they steamed into San Pedro's inadequate harbor, a shallow lagoon on the lee side of the island, they could hear a rinky-dink piano going full blast in the hung-over pre-dawn light. They found out why the stolen yacht had a banged up screw when they hit another boulder of brain coral with the fortunately slowly spinning blades. It was light enough now, to just make out the ramshackle little settlement. San Pedro looked like stale tobacco smoke smells—gray and fuzzy. Most of the roofing was palm thatch. A few local bigshots had corrugated iron. Nobody rated two stories. A snaggletooth line of sea grape, gumbo limbo and palmetto rose behind the town. Gaston said a shot fired into the tree tops would splash in the sea to the east. But that was because San Pedro occupied a wasp waist. The cay was over five miles wide in other spots. All told, Ambergris Cay had over twice the dimension and hence over four times the area of New York's better known Manhattan Island. Since the cay had perhaps a fraction of one percent of Manhattan's population, it was mostly covered with uninhabited scrub—trees, where the soil was deep enough, thorn and cactus where it wasn't. Visitors to the American Tropics always acted surprised to see cactus in the warm muggy parts. But cactus was an American plant, and where it might or might not grow depended more on how much water was retained by the soil than how much fell from the sky. Like the mainland to the north, Ambergris Cay was elevated sea bottom and its coral-stone soil was dry as hell between showers.

At Gaston's suggestion, Captain Gringo made for the one frail wooden pier running out to reasonably deep draft. He could see most of the small fishing vessels were beached on the gently sloping strand. As they approached, a tall thin black ambled out along the pier, waving his straw sombrero. Gaston moved forward to heave a line ashore as Captain Gringo reversed the screw. The helpful townsman caught the line and whipped it around a mooring post. Captain Gringo threw him a stern line; he did the same, and they were fast to the docks, so he cut the engine. The guy who'd helped was standing there, like he expected something. So Captain Gringo waved him aboard. As he was handing the guy a few contavos, Gaston came aft, grinned and held out his hand, saying, "*Eh bien*—Cockpit Calvin is alive and well and hiding out on Ambergris Cay."

The black laughed, shook hands with Gaston, and replied, "I thought they hung you a long time ago, Mon."

Gaston introduced Cockpit Calvin to Captain Gringo, assuring each that the other was a rogue, and hence could be trusted to know the code of the knockaround guy. Captain Gringo explained why they'd come to the cay. Cockpit Calvin said, "I'm in, Mon. I'd join anybody and do anything to get off this beach. But you'll have a hard time finding others as willing as me to work for provision and passage. Are you sure you have no money at all, Mon? You can trust me to keep secrets."

Captain Gringo said, "I'll take Gaston's word on you, Cockpit. We're really having this war on a shoestring. There might be some loot at the end of the rainbow. El Cazador is supposed to be rich and he must keep at least a few good cigars around his house."

"You go and talk to the others then, Mon. I say I'm in, but Gaston can tell you I am restless. Did I have a good-looking momma or did I even know where there was a decent turtle beach on this fool island, I wouldn't join you. We've heard tell about El Cazador, here. He ain't just rich. He's one crazy hombre malo!"

Captain Gringo said he wanted to talk to the other beach bums ashore and, since he needed Gaston to introduce him around and cover his back, he asked Cockpit Calvin to keep an eye on the vessel. Cockpit Calvin said he had nothing better to do, was up for the day, and had no place better to go. So they left him on guard with the high-powered rifle from El Cazador's stateroom across his knees and orders to stay out of the bottles and the one broad they were leaving in his charge.

Ynez was still sleeping down below, but Captain Gringo left her a note so she wouldn't be startled when she awoke to find herself alone with a stranger. As he and Gaston walked ashore, armed only with the pistols under their jackets, Gaston assured him Cockpit Calvin could be trusted around white women. Captain Gringo grimaced and replied, "I wouldn't have left the schooner, the girl, and the Maxim in his care if I'd thought he was likely to run off with any of them."

"Ah, *oui*, les boats et les broads can be replaced, but machineguns are *très* hard to find."

"Never mind all that. How trustworthy are the guys we're going to meet?"

"That's hard to say, Dick. Some, like Calvin, back there, are just rogues like you and me. Others would murder their mothers for a drink."

Nobody was actually attacking their mothers as Gaston and the tinkle of that off-key piano led Captain Gringo into the biggest saloon on the cay. But a couple of naked ladies were having one hell of a brawl in the middle of the floor as the customers, male and female, watched with various expressions ranging from interest to ennui. One of the girls was white and the other black. The bruises showed better on the white girl's bare hide, but she looked as if she were winning. She had the Negress down and was banging her head on the floor. Gaston sniffed and said it was a fake match staged for entertainment. Captain Gringo didn't comment, but tended to agree. Neither of them had bitten off the other's nose or nipples, so they probably weren't really serious.

Gaston led him down to the end of the bar where an

even blacker and more heroically proportioned woman wearing red hair and a red dress sat watching the fight with a bemused expression on her face. She looked tough enough to take both combatants on, but she was sort of pretty, in a weird way. Gaston introduced her as Pegeen O'Hara, last of the Black Irish.

The owner of the nameless saloon laughed, "Gaston, you old basser, the last I heard of you, they said you'd been sentenced to be shot up Mexico way."

"I was," Gaston said. "That's where I met Dick Walker here. You may have heard of him as Captain Gringo."

Pegeen smiled and said, "I have that. Put her there me bucko, and do you have a gorl at the moment?"

He laughed and said he admitted both crimes. The big red-headed black woman sighed and said, "Oh, hell, I was planning on a celebration this evening, too. But if you boyos didn't come here to get drunk or seek other creature comforts, we'd best go in me office to plot."

She led them through a beaded curtain and down a short hallway to what she called her office. It looked more like a boudoir lined with red velvet. Pegeen must have noticed their reaction. She said, "What could be after bringing the two of yez to such a dreadful place?"

Gaston gave Captain Gringo the floor and Pegeen listened until he'd brought her up to date. Then she whistled softly and said, "Jasus, I might have known a friend of Gaston's would be mad, too. El Cazador is known by repute in these parts. You'll have a time gathering a crew to fight him and his private army at the wages you're offering."

"We thought some of the guys here might welcome a chance to see some action just for the hell of it. So far we've recruited one islander who's willing to come along for an outside chance on loot."

The redhead shrugged and said, "They say that mad Spaniard's rich, but they say he's a mighty big boo, too.

Aside from being forted up on his own plantation with at least a score of hired guns, he's supposed to have an in with the damned auld rurales. So even if yez could take him out, yez'd have to run like hell before yez could really do a thoughtful job of looting. He'd be a fool to keep his fortune stuffed in his own mattress when it can be earning interest in a bank. Faith, I bank in Corozal meself."

"Sure, but don't you keep at least enough on hand for current expenses between boats?"

"Och, of course I do. But me point is that nobody robbing me out here on the cay at gunpoint would get any real money. The true value to be found at most plantations is the land and crops themselves. You'll play hell liquidating either with them dreadful rurales shooting at you."

Captain Gringo nodded and said, "I agree it'll have to be hit and run, but the bastard really needs to be hit, Pegeen. You folks here on the cay aren't really safe from El Cazador if he decides to hunt a bit further afield than usual."

She said, "I've heard of the value El Cazador places on human life, Dick. But we're in better shape than them poor Mexican peones to the north. You see, the Indians of Quintana Roo ain't in good with the Mexican government. They keep rising against Mexican rule. They must be part Irish, like me. At any rate, Mexico don't care if El Cazador weeds out the dark side of the population for them. But here on the cay we're under British rule, and while I'm not that fond of the auld queen, she's fair dacent about protecting her subjects from outright murder."

Captain Gringo started to say he'd noticed El Cazador had been reasonably cautious, for a bloodthirsty butcher, in Corozal and Belize. Then he frowned and said, "I just remembered a message we intercepted. El Cazador is wanted by the British authorities. There might be a reward on the bugger, if we could deliver him to the royal governor in Belize!"

Gaston snorted in disgust and asked, "*Merde,* how would we collect the reward on another outlaw without someone collecting the reward on *us*?"

But Pegeen O'Hara said that was just a technicality and that the reward angle sounded interesting. She added, "Sure, you'd need at least a dozen men and it would still be two-to-one or more. But yez have a machinegun and in God's truth, there ain't a score of hard cases here on the cay that would be dumb enough as well. You'll need boyos with their own guns as well as adventurous natures."

She shot a glance at the fancy French clock on her dressing table and added, "At this hour, dacent sober gintry would be out fishing or beach combing. You'd not want anyone still slugabed at sunrise in the tropics. For if a man means to be active at all, he does his daylight chores well before the noon siesta time. That's when you'll find the boyos you're after back in town and ready to listen to you. Pay no attention to the drunks out front. It's men who like hunting and fishing that you'd want to take along, if you can talk a sober lad into it at all!"

They said they'd come back later and headed back to rejoin Ynez and Cockpit Calvin on the schooner. It was now broad daylight but still cool. The lagoon lay on the lee side of the cay so the water was glassy smooth as the schooner brooded out at the end of the pier like a big black hen. There was no sign of either their new recruit or the Basque girl on deck as they strode out to the schooner.

Ynez could still be sleeping, but it was a hell of a way to stand deck watch. Captain Gringo called out as he and Gaston approached. Nothing. He drew his revolver. Gaston said not to be so dramatic. Then as they got closer, Gaston drew his, too. Captain Gringo said, "Cover me. I'll go aboard first."

He did so. Then, as he saw what lay on the cockpit deck, half hidden by the wheel-box, the hairs on the back of his neck tingled and he froze in place. Cockpit Calvin lay dead in the cockpit. Captain Gringo didn't have to check his pulse to know he was dead. Someone had cut the tall Negro's head off!

There had to be some way of getting below without going through a hatch, but there wasn't, and both Ynez and their only heavy weapon had been left down there.

He waved Gaston aboard and, as Gaston spotted the beheaded black and made the sign of the cross, Captain Gringo went below, and went fast. There's no smart way to sneak through a doorway when a gun might be waiting for one on the far side, but easing in slow is the dumb way. He leaped to the floor of the salon, skipping the ladder rungs and crabbing sideways to cover the interior from the corner on one knee. The salon was deserted. He moved forward—aging a year—as he checked out each possible ambush. But there was nobody else aboard—including Ynez.

The preserved head in the closet was missing, too. He found the pilot light on under the boiler in the engine room. Apparently nothing else but the gun they'd left with poor Calvin had been tampered with. When he went topside and reported this to Gaston, the older Frenchman shrugged and said, "*Eh bien,* it's his boat in the first place. He seems to have only come for a few personal belongings."

"Goddamn it, Ynez doesn't belong to him!"

"*Oui,* but maybe he is too crazy to get his own girl. What about the Maxim, Dick?"

It was a good question. Captain Gringo stepped over Cockpit Calvin's sprawled legs, moved some seat cushions out of the way, and raised the lid of the seat to say, with a relieved sigh, "He missed it." Then he noticed a folded slip of paper tucked into the bolt slot and took it out, opened it, and read, "My esteemed prey: I have left my yacht in your care, since you seem to have used up most of the fuel. I have left you this weapon to make our next encounter more interesting. But really, Captain Gringo, can't you do better than this? You are running in circles like a mere rabbit. Frankly, I expected more from an old Apache fighter. I grow weary of our little game. Accordingly, I shall end it, whether you start making it interesting or not, by the end of the week. I have other affairs to attend to, and hunting you is to yawn."

There was no signature—none was needed. He asked Gaston, "How many days to the end of the week?" and Gaston answered, "Three, why?"

Captain Gringo handed him the note. Gaston read it, nodded, and said, "Obviously, this was designed to rattle us. He must be afraid we're heading for his plantation headquarters and he wanted to make us run somewhere else, non?"

"He wants us to come play in his yard, you mean. That's the only reason he had for taking Ynez alive. He'd have left her dead with this other poor slob, here, if he just wanted to be a scary bastard."

"We don't know Ynez is still alive, Dick."

"She might be, and El Cazador's expecting us to try and rescue her. Can't you read *anything* between the lines?"

"I was hoping you couldn't. *Sacre bleu,* Dick, this is getting *très* serious. Not only are we outgunned *très formidable* by an ogre in his own lair with the police on his side, but he knows we are coming and, now that they have Ynez, he knows our plans in detail!"

"Yeah, we'll have to assume Ynez will talk. I know I might if I were in her shoes. But meanwhile, let's see if anyone on shore spotted the snatch. We weren't gone long, so how far could they have gotten by now?"

"Home, if they arrived in another boat. Otherwise they would most naturally still be somewhere here on Ambergris Cay!"

They hurried ashore. After that, things slowed down. They walked up the strand to where a couple of black kids were casting minnow nets in the shallows. Captain Gringo gave them a couple of coins and they still said they hadn't seen anything, the little bastards.

One volunteered he was sure he'd have noticed another ocean-going craft out there by the schooner, now that he thought about it. He said, "I didn't notice you gen'mens goin' and comin' on the pier. Folks is always goin' and comin' on the pier. But I likes to look at *boats.* I'm sure I seen no other boat out there on the water since we got here."

"Okay, how long have you been here?"

"Lessee, since first light, I reckons. Ain't that right, Willy?" "Sure," the other kid said. "Ever'body knows you got to git up early to catch ol' minnow fishes. They's already headin' back to deep water, the mammy jammers!"

The first boy pointed at their buckets and said, "We got us some bait before sunrise, Mistuh. Ain't no boats come into the lagoon since then."

The two soldiers of fortune exchanged glances. Gaston nodded. The sun had been up when they'd left Ynez and the vessel in Cockpit Calvin's charge. But as Captain Gringo started legging on up the beach, Gaston demanded, "Where are we marching in such a *dramatique* fashion, my young and restless?"

Captain Gringo growled, "North, of course. There's only a narrow channel between this cay and the mainland."

"True, but the north end of the island is a good twelve miles or more from here in the first place and we are only armed with our pistols in the second! If you mean to track down God-knows-how-many in the shrubbery you are advancing on, can't we at least go back to the schooner and get a couple of rifles?"

"We don't have time. Even if they're on foot, they have one hell of a lead on us. Besides, a pistol's good enough, fighting in brush. You'd better stay here, Gaston. I can move faster and quieter on my own, no offense, and unless one of us has a chat with the locals about Cockpit Calvin, we could come walking back into a pretty unreasonable scene."

"*Oui,* it seems a good idea to get him ashore and hose down the deck before the sun gets really hot. But I've a better idea. Why don't we *both* turn back? Be reasonable, Dick. You may be doing just what El Cazador wants by charging into the shrubbery alone and lightly armed!"

"I already thought of that. Fuck him. He says he's looking for a showdown with me. That's the one thing I can agree on with the lunatic. If I'm not back by siesta time, start without me."

The few inhabitants of Ambergris Cay grew a patch of produce here and there in the white patchy soil. A mile north of town they didn't even do that. The brush was mostly sea grape and thorn to shoulder height, with palmetto and gumbo limbo offering most of the meager shade. The coral sand was too dry to hold foot prints. He could see where people had walked one way or the other an hour or a week ago; but singling out any particular spoor was impossible. On the other hand, he'd learned in his Indian fighting days with the old Tenth Cav that you seldom tracked a quarry far enough to matter by sniffing at footprints like a dog. You figured the lay of the land and where the bastards had to be headed. Then you went there. Fast. The advantage a good tracker had was sometimes that the trackee was wasting time trying to cover his tracks. Captain Gringo knew the cay narrowed to a narrow point to the north, facing Mexico across the narrow channel between Ambergris Cay and the mainland. El Cazador and anyone with him probably had a raft or rowboat waiting there. He knew he had to be walking faster than anyone could carry a woman, even if they'd knocked her out. He might have missed a horse or mule print in the soft white soil, but by now he'd have seen at least a couple of turds if they had a beast of burden packing for them.

There was one other way the bastards could have meant to work it. Another sea going vessel could be waiting for them at the *south* end of the cay. But a fifty-fifty chance was better than the odds Geronimo had offered, and Geronimo was a P.O.W. at Fort Sill right now, so what the hell.

The island widened as he bulled north. He didn't make sweeps from side to side as it was too far across to cover everything. He'd catch up if they bee-lined north and he wouldn't if they didn't. He thought about the odds on them holing up in the scrub and letting him pass. He hoped they wouldn't. They had no way of knowing one man would be dumb enough to be trailing them alone. Assuming El Cazador was the skilled woodsman everyone said he was, holing up sounded dumb. Even if he hadn't gotten Ynez to tell him by now, El Cazador had to know he and Gaston wouldn't have come here unless they expected to meet friends, and the cay men were reputed to be tough, too.

No, the crazy Basque's best bet was a straight run for home plate. So Captain Gringo bulled through some innocent-looking shrubbery that left his shirt filled with little stinging nettles. He walked around a clump of glandular cactus and almost stepped on a glandular looking snake before he saw it in time and leaped to one side as the bushmaster struck. He pointed his revolver at the recoiling snake and muttered, "Okay, live and let live, but you're not supposed to *be* out here on the offshore islands, pal!"

He moved on, still tingling over that unexpected encounter with the bushmaster, as he thought how often the wilder forms of life down here in the tropics had forgotten to read the natural history books. A guy could get hurt in these parts, going by the books. Somehow sharks wound up in fresh water streams and lakes, while crocodilians somehow wound up in salty waters science said they weren't supposed to survive in. He ducked his head under a tree limb just as a bullet spanged bark off it—from his side!

He hit the white dirt and rolled as another round gouted flour-fine dust from the surface he'd just rolled away from. Then he wriggled into a clump of Spanish Bayonet, ignoring the dagger-like leaves trying to blind him, as he heard another round whizz over him like an enraged metal insect. He still didn't know where the shots were coming from!

The shots had sounded high powered. The guy who'd fired was using the new smokeless powder. Captain Gringo eased forward through the Spanish Bayonet on his belly, gun muzzle sweeping with his eyes as he explored the salad greenery all about him. Not a leaf was moving. He yelled, "Come out and fight, you son-of-a-bitch!" But there was no answer. It figured. He wouldn't have been dumb enough to expose *his* position, so why should El Cazador?

He realized he'd yelled in English. The note and a couple of people had told him the lunatic spoke English. But maybe he didn't take it as personal as his own lingo? Captain Gringo didn't know how to cuss a guy out in Basque. So, in Spanish, he tried, "I would spit in your mother's milk, if whores gave milk. So I spit in the puss of her rotting tits!"

Nothing. Not even a shot that might give the bastard's position away. Remembering another suspicion about the bloodthirsty Basque, Captain Gringo called out, "Hey, Mariposa, what's the matter, have you caught a dose with your mouth?"

A rifle round whizzed just above Captain Gringo's spine, from the wrong direction! The son-of-a-bitch had circled around behind him! He rolled, crushing the Spanish Bayonet and ignoring the stabbing leaf points as he rose on one elbow, spotted the faint blue haze of smokeless powder against spinach green, and fired his .38 at it before rolling the other way and, yeah, not being there when a high-powered slug spanged into the spot he'd been rolling toward! He fired at the sound, hoping the bastard would at least flinch, as he did a backward somersault to land belly down facing the last shots, as he crawfished deeper into the brush feeling his way with his boots and hoping not to kick any important snakes. At times like these, a guy had to consider the odds. A bushmaster fang in the ankle took longer to kill you than a bullet in the head.

His feet encountered a fallen palmetto log as he slid his length over it like a flattened out slug going the wrong way and, with improved cover, thumbed fresh rounds into his .38 before he called out, sarcastically, "Hey, how's about a great big kiss, if I bend over and spread my cheeks?"

No answer. Aware now that El Cazador liked to circle, Captain Gringo coiled like a snake himself, and kept an eye on his rear approaches as well when he cried, "I see you now, you limp-wristed clown! How come you have your pants on? I thought all Basques took it in the ass!"

Nothing. He tried, "Hey, no shit, are you really a Basque? I met some Basques in the States one time. They didn't look like you. They looked like *men!*"

That didn't work either. He heard something skittering in the dry leaves, not far away. He tensed. It turned out to be a little fence lizard, going someplace in a hurry. Captain Gringo watched the brush behind it as the lizard came his way, froze and cocked its tiny head to keep an eye on whatever the hell he was. Captain Gringo didn't move. The lizard lost interest and slithered off to eat an ant or something. Nothing followed it out of the brush. He called, "This sure is getting tedious, Montalban. Let's talk."

There was no answer. So Captain Gringo cussed him some more with the same results. He began to wonder if he were alone in this neck of the woods. He didn't move. Thinking like that got a lot of soldiers killed.

The trick in one of these Mexican Standoffs was to wait as long as the other guy, then wait a couple of minutes longer. El Cazador was an old hand at this game, so he'd know it too. Captain Gringo decided to shut up and let El Cazador worry if *he* was hunkered doggo while the other side moved out or around him. War was a bore, when one did it right.

It felt like a million years, but his pocket watch said nothing had happened for the better part of an hour when Captain Gringo decided enough was enough. This time he didn't taunt his unseen enemy as he gingerly shifted positions. Knowing El Cazador was at least as good a hunter as he was, the tall American didn't try to think up a smart way to crawl. He just moved off at random until he knew he was out of rifle range from El Cazador's last likely position. Naturally he'd moved slowly enough to make sure nobody was following him. He crawled under some low growing thorn on his belly and gingerly rose to his feet on the far side for a better view all round. Nobody blew his head off. On the other hand, he saw nothing but a lot of unpleasant vegetation. He started to work north again. Then he checked the time once more, shrugged, muttered, "Fuck it," and turned back toward San Pedro.

Putting himself in El Cazador's place, he saw what the game had been. El Cazador had kept him pinned down with bullets and his own caution for over an hour while his henchmen carried Ynez, dead or alive, on toward the point. There was no way he was about to catch up, unless he just threw caution to the winds and ran after them, blindly, through the scrub.

With the deadly El Cazador covering their trail, armed with a smokeless high-powered rifle and the initiative, a blind bull charge could take years off a guy's life.

Captain Gringo felt shitty about giving up, but there were times a good soldier had to, and this was one of them. El Cazador had won this round. They might have killed Ynez. They might be planning to kill her later. There was nothing he could do about it right now. Meanwhile he was hot and thirsty and the sooner he and Gaston recruited some help, the sooner they could try for a rematch on better terms.

A palm frond rustled like a rattlesnake's tail behind him. Captain Gringo dove headfirst into a clump of sea grape and rolled out the other side, licking dust and the dry taste of fear from his bared teeth as he lay on his gut with gun muzzle and wary gray eyes trained on the scrub. He warned himself, "Steady, now. Mommy and Daddy are right downstairs and lots of things go bump in the night besides the Boogy Man."

He was sweating harder than the temperature really called for. It was dry and musty rather than really hot in the shady scrub he was beginning to view with the same enthusiasm as a fly views a spider's web. He felt trapped. He wanted out. It had to be easier to breathe, out in the open where a guy could see another with a gun at least ten paces away. The still air at ground level tasted like dusty straw in a haunted hay loft. Where in hell had the trade winds gone? Oh yeah, up against the cobalt blue sky a few branches were moving. He heard the same sinister rustle and stiffened, heart pounding. Then he located the source of the sound, cursed, and smiled sheepishly. The gentle morning trades were swinging a dead dried frond across the rough bark of a taller palm.

He got to his feet and moved on, muttering for allowing himself to be spooked by mere jungle noises. He knew that was what El Cazador wanted. Any hunter knows spooked game makes foolish moves in panic. El Cazador was used to hunting people who were afraid of him. That was why he worked so hard to scare his victims. It gave him an edge.

But as Captain Gringo walked back to the outskirts of San Pedro, he'd calmed enough to wonder, "Edge to do what?"

There was more to El Cazador's game than everyone accepted at face value. There had to be a weanie. Sure, tracking down and killing poor scared natives was probably a lot of laughs. But El Cazador had loyal followers and enjoyed the protection and friendship of at least the local rurales up in Quintana Roo. Ergo he couldn't be a frothing-at-the-mouth, rolling-on-the-floor nut. To run with a pack, even a pack of brutal bastards, a guy had to have *some* self-control!

El Cazador had a noticcablc yellow streak, too, if that had been El Cazador he'd just tangled with back there. For a guy who claimed to be a mighty macho hunter, he'd sure acted unwilling to go *mano-a-mano* when he'd found himself alone with his chosen prey and holding the better hand.

Or had he? Putting himself in El Cazador's boots, Captain Gringo knew that if he'd been laying in wait with a scope sighted, high-powered rifle the guy he'd been laying for would be dead about now. Unless all those stories about El Cazador's odd hobby were bullshit, he was pussyfooting around. Nobody hunted human prey long enough to matter unless he was good. Damned good. The whole point of such a grotesque sport was that a human being was the most dangerous critter one could hunt. Sure, lots of poor scared guys would just run like rabbits 'til El Cazador tracked them down. But not all of them.

Even naked savages and Mexican peones wanted to live, and some of them would have been skilled woodsmen and reasonably tough and cunning. El Cazador had to be even slyer than his prey. So, okay, what was sly about all this bullshit? What was El Cazador expecting him and Gaston to do about his cat and mouse warnings and near misses?

Captain Gringo tried those other boots again and could only come up with three answers. He knew that if he warned a reasonably rugged couple of guys that he was after them, they would either run away, hide, or come after him. By now El Cazador had to have figured out he and Gaston were neither running nor hiding enough to matter. If El Cazador was worried about them coming after him, he sure had picked a funny way to discourage them. You don't kidnap a guy's girl and brag about it to his face if you don't want him coming after you. It had been a naked dare. El Cazador wanted them on his own hunting preserve.

Okay, why? To kill them where the local law wouldn't pester him about it? That wouldn't work. El Cazador wasn't worried about killing *other* people on British soil. The Royal Constabulary would hang him just as high for murdering Cockpit Calvin and kidnapping Ynez Bilbao. Hell, they'd do it *faster!* Neither the black beachcomber nor the Basque girl had wanted papers out on them. Captain Gringo and Gaston were both wanted criminals almost anyone could gun with impunity in broad daylight, almost anywhere.

"That's it," he decided, with a grim little smile. The

saloon was in sight and he saw Gaston waiting for him under the sheet-metal overhang by the doorway. He joined Hell, they'd do it *faster*! Neither the black beachcomber the boat and we buried Cockpit Calvin. I see you are still alive, but empty handed."

Captain Gringo waited until they'd gone in and bellied up to the bar before he said, "It's the rewards on us. El Cazador can't collect on our heads south of the border because the Brits are after him, too. On the other hand, El Presidente Diaz and Los Rurales would pat him on the back a lot, and give him the money, if he nailed us on Mexican soil."

Gaston asked the West Indian barkeep for rum and coconut water and Captain Gringo said he'd have the same. Then Gaston said, "*Eh bein,* it works. It explains the preserved human head in his closet, too. The victim looked Mexican. What will you bet he was wanted in Mexico?"

"No bet. El Cazador's not just a sadistic maniac. He likes to kill people. But he likes to make his hobby pay, too. In Africa he made expenses by working with Arab slaves. Over on this side of the pond he keeps in good with the Mexican rurales by sharing occasional rewards with them."

"I hate bounty hunters. One detail still eludes me, Dick. The papers on you and me read dead or alive. I see why he didn't want us running further away from the Mexican line, but is he not still trying to do it the hard way? Had he killed us in Belize and simply carried our heads back as proof . . ."

"Ouch. That sounds uncomfortable. I think I know the answer, too. You remember all those trains we blew up when we were helping those Mexican rebels a while back?"

Gaston grinned and said, "*Mais oui,* and no doubt El Presidente Diaz does, too. That is why he'd no doubt pay well for our handsome heads on his desk."

"He'd pay more for us alive. Aside from having a personal hard-on for us, Diaz and his torturers would like to chat with us about the Mexican rebels we share a mutual interest in. *That's* what all this cat and mouse bullshit is. El Cazador wants us to come after him on his own turf so that he and his rurale pals can take us *alive*!"

Gaston took a sip of his drink, pronounced it dreadful, and suggested, "In that case, let us fool them. We have the boat. I've found a handful of rogues who'd be willing to crew her, if we were going anywhere else. So let's go anywhere else."

"Can't. El Cazador has Ynez."

"*Merde alors,* let us be *practique*! She's not the only woman in the world and even if she were, she's probably dead by now. Can't you see El Cazador is trying to *bait* you, Dick?"

"Yeah, he's doing pretty good, too. You may be right about the girl. I know you're right about him expecting us to beard him in his den. But we have to do it, so let's figure out the best way, right?"

"*Sacre bleu,* there is no best way, you species of idiot! El Cazador holds all the aces! He has the local populace terrified and under his thumb. He has the local law in his hip pocket. Ynez said his plantation house is built like a fort. And he knows we're coming!"

Gaston took another sip and added, "That is, he *thinks* we're coming. I, too, am the *très* tricky tactition. Let's trick him good, by sailing south and leaving him to the devil, hein?"

Captain Gringo took a sip of rum and coconut water before he agreed. "You're right," he admitted. "This stuff is awful. The devil isn't after El Cazador. I am. Call me quixotic, but I can't share the same planet with a monster like El Cazador. He just murdered a knockaround pal and kidnapped a friendly gal. Some of his bounty hunting makes sadistic sense, but he still shoots little people just for target practice, and I don't like his rurale hunting companions all that much, either. You don't have to tag along if it's too big a boo for you, Gaston. But I'm going to nail that prick if it's the last thing I do!"

"*Merde alors,* it probably will be, but count me in. If I don't come along to keep an eye on you, you'll surely do something foolish."

Captain Gringo smiled down at Gaston and said, "Now you're talking. Let's make some plans. How do you think we ought to go about taking the son-of-a-bitch out, Gaston?"

Gaston shrugged and replied, "I've no idea. As I said, El Cazador holds all the aces. We stand to get killed or captured no matter how we plan it, but what can I say? I have no older and wiser head to keep *me* from acting foolish!"

Gaston left to see if he could hunt down some more deck hands as Captain Gringo waited in the saloon in hopes of recruiting more serious help, when and if the local toughs came in to cool off at noon. La Siesta wasn't official in British Crown Colonies, but any white or West Indian who'd been south of Cancer long enough to skip wearing a tie knew enough to seek shade from noon to three. He found himself almost alone in the late morning lull. The only other customers looked like hopeless drunks, so he didn't bother with them. He stood at the bar, nursing a claro and a more reasonable rum and tonic as the sun rose higher and the flies buzzed faster. The redheaded black Irish Pegeen O'Hara who came out from her so-called office, seemed surprised and pleased to see him there. He was surprised and pleased to see her, too, as she'd changed into a thin red silk kimono. It was open above the waist sash. Pegeen had a fantastic pair of egg-plant black breasts. She said, "Faith and you're just the man I want to talk to. Come back to me office. For it's a private matter."

He followed her, enjoying the view from behind, too. That red silk was awfully thin. Pegeen ushered him into her red velvet lined lair and locked the door as she waved him to a seat on her bed. Then she moved over to the dresser and started pouring drinks from what looked like a cologne bottle, saying, "I have to hide the good stuff. Have a snort of the real poteen. It'll put hair on your chest."

He tasted the Irish malt liquor and resisted an impulse to remark it could remove the lining of one's gullet, too. She was obviously trying to be friendly and he sure needed friends right now. Pegeen sat down beside him and patted his knee as one of her own long, shapely, black and naked limbs popped into view. She said, "I've been brooding over the way thim rascals trated poor Cockpit Calvin. He was a damned auld protestant, but a dacent man for all that and, well, I know you won't believe this, but I've a bit of African blood on me sainted mother's side."

"Really? I hadn't noticed."

"Och, cut your blarney. The point I'm making is that I want to help you get that dreadful Mexican, El Cazador. You and auld Gaston can't even man that boat, without extra hands."

"Yeah, but, no offense, we're not recruiting females. We need at least a dozen men who can handle a gun as well as a schooner, Pegeen."

"Och, I know that. Did you think I'd leave me darling pub to go off to war with yez? The help I'm offering is more practical. I've got a few barrels of fuel oil I can give yez. I've got a dozen Winchesters and the ammo to go with them. For I own the general store here in town as well as this house of ill repute. How do you like the deal so far?"

"Very much. But how are we to pay you, Pegeen?" We're running low on funds and we can't leave the schooner as security."

"Jasus, did I say anything about being paid? It's a rich woman I am, and I know you boyos are about broke. That takes us to the second part of this discussion."

She slid her other dark leg out of the open kimono, leaving damned little to the imagination as she took a wad of pound notes from under her red lace garter and handed it to him, saying, "In a little while the boyos you need will start drifting in. They're tough hard men, but they'll laugh at yez if asked to go adventuring without at least a little front money."

He looked down at the hefty wad in amazement and said, "Jesus, Pegeen. I'm not about to say I can't take this. But how the hell do you expect us to pay you back?"

She shrugged and said, "Och, I water the drinks out front. Don't worry about paying me back. I know you will if you can. I only wish I could go with yez to fight them dreadful Mexicans. But I know I'd just be in the way. So take what help I can give yez and let's say no more about it."

She looked away, but he'd spotted the tear running down her cheek. So he placed a gentle hand on her shoulder and murmured, "Hey, Pegeen?"

"Och, pay no attention, Dick. It's the Irish in me acting daft. Would you be after leaving now? We'll talk about the guns and other supplies later. Right now I mean to have me a good cry."

He held her closer and said, "Tell me about it." So she turned to bury her face against his chest as she sobbed, "It's so little I can do and I feel so guilty about Cockpit Calvin."

"You mean, he was your boyfriend?"

"Och, that'll be the day. I'm not *that* black. But, sure, that's part of the guilt I feel, for the poor thing acted fond of me and I did treat him cruel one time. You see, when he first came to the cay he made advances and, well, I called him a forward nigger and worse. Do you think he still hated me when they were killing him, Dick?"

"I doubt it. Cockpit Calvin was a knockaround guy. He was no kid. We've all been turned down by a pretty girl in our time. Nobody but a jerk-off nurses a grudge about it."

He noticed she was toying with a button on his shirt as she sighed and said, "I hope you're right. I suppose I'm more sensitive about the darker branches of me family tree than I thought. For when I heard they'd treated poor black Calvin so cruel, a terrible rage came over me to me own surprise. How would you account for that, Dick? I'm a woman of color, as anyone can see, but I've never taken the matter seriously before."

"Hell, everyone has a right to get upset when someone they know gets his head lopped off. Calvin was a good guy and a fellow islander. I'd be more surprised if it *hadn't* upset you."

"You don't think it's tom-toms beating in me nigger blood, then?"

"Don't call yourself names. Don't worry about normal human feelings, either. I think you'd have been just as upset and just as willing to help if they'd murdered one of your other customers, white, black, or in between."

She laughed softly and said, "You know, you're right? I've a softer heart for the boyos than I like to let them know. A woman in me position has to keep most men at a distance, but that gives no stranger the right to cut heads off me customers!"

She had a second button unfastened and her hand was inside his shirt, shyly sliding up and down his belly. He pulled her a little closer but warned her, "If you're trying to keep me at a distance you're going about it all wrong."

She said, "You already have lots of hair on your chest, I see. You probably find me too dark for your taste, but if you don't, you're not an Ambergris man, so we don't have to worry about gossip and . . ."

He kissed her to shut her up as they fell back across the bed. She moaned in pleased surprise and went to work in earnest on his buttons as he untied the sash around her waist. Her kimono fell open to either side. He was open down the front, too, so he rolled atop her with her eggplant black breasts against his naked chest, her junoesque black torso pressed to his belly, and their more important parts making contact between her wide spread ebony thighs. As he entered her he could tell she hadn't been getting it regular, recently, but from the way she started moving her hips he knew she had, a lot, in the past.

She was a warm-natured Earth Mother who had no inhibitions, once she got going. She came before he did. And then he fired a round into her, surprised at how good it felt to just let himself go in a hot, uncomplicated, and very tight partner. When they came up for air, Pegeen suggested it would be nicer if they stripped completely. So they did. It took him a few moments longer, since he had more to take off. Pegeen rose from her open kimono like a dark Venus rising from the waves and stepped over to her dresser to adjust the mirror. He didn't ask why. When she returned to the bed she got on top. They looked sort of silly in the mirror. But she seemed to get an added kick out of it as she bounced up and down in a rotary teasing way that gave a literal meaning to the verb "to screw." It felt like she was trying to wring his dong out like a dishrag. But no dishrag ever had it so good.

After they'd come that way, they settled down to a long, friendly daylight orgy, with a pornographic-mirror show to add spice to the proceedings. When they finally ran out of positions and breath, she shared a cigar with him and he braced himself for the usual post orgasmic bullshit. But Pegeen was great about that, too. She didn't ask if he still respected her or if he wanted to come home and have some of her mother's chicken soup. She just cuddled close, told him he'd made her very happy, and asked him if he wanted to sleep a while before going out to meet the boyos. He took a drag on the claro, placed it between her moist lips, and said, "Want to, but I can't. I'd like to spend the next few years in this bed, Pegeen. But I've got another date with a guy in Mexico."

She giggled and toyed with his sated shaft as she said, "Och, I think I should be jealous. Is it true El Cazador's effeminate?"

"I don't know. Nothing about him makes much sense. An English girl he married for some strange reason says he never touched her. But he did marry her. So if he's a mariposa he doesn't want it to get around."

"Do you think he'll ravage that Spanish girl they kidnapped off your boat?"

"She's Basque, not Spanish, and it's not my boat, it's his schooner. I don't think he kidnapped Ynez Bilbao to rape her."

"Why? Was she that ugly?"

"No. But his English wife was as pretty and must have been more willing, before she found out he was ga-ga. I'd feel better about them holding Ynez if I didn't suspect the guy was a nasty homosexual. Rape is nasty, too, but at least she'd probably live through it. There's no telling what the hell a sadistic queer would do to a female prisoner. So I don't think I'd better stay the night here. What time is it?"

"It's early yet. The boyos will be out front 'til after three and I feel signs of life in this dreadful weapon I'm holding. So let's finish this darling cigar and see what comes up. I can see that whatever El Cazador is, *you* like gorls."

"I'd be in trouble if I didn't," he chuckled. "You seem pretty normal, too."

"Ay, I've never understood that other business. What do you suppose paple like El Cazador get out of their queer notions, Dick?"

"Beats me. I've never thought of a thing I could do to another man that I couldn't do better to a woman."

"Well, I have heard it said thim sissy lads take it in the mouth and other naughty places."

"So what? Don't you girls have them, too?"

"I can't spake for others," she laughed, "but I do. Would you like to come in me all three ways, Darling?"

"Does a rooster flap his wings and crow? But what would you get out of it, Pegeen?"

"Experience? Lay back and let me watch us in the mirror as I indulge in grand crimes against nature!"

So he did, and it looked wild as hell to lay there smoking a cigar and watching their reflections in the mirror as Pegeen crouched over him, rump raised, and aimed at the mirror, while she gave him an inspired French lesson. He enjoyed it up to full arousal, but didn't want to waste an orgasm between her tonsils as he stared at the reflection of her pulsating vaginal lips in the mirror. He snuffed out the smoke and asked her to stop. But she didn't. She sucked harder and made him come that way as he stared wistfully at her other kissy lips. Then, as he lay weakly panting but still erect, Pegeen raised her head with a roguish grin, and said, "That was fun" and climbed atop him again. He was willing. He assumed she was going to screw him some more the way they'd been doing it. Then, as he felt her shoe-horning the tip into unfamiliar territory, he frowned and asked, "Are you sure you know what you're doing? That doesn't feel like the right place, Honey."

She settled her weight gingerly down on him as he popped inside her anal muscles and slid even deeper. She gasped and said, "Och, Jasus, I think I might be committing suicide. Do you like the way that feels?"

"Yeah, but what about you?"

"I'm not sure. As I said, it's a new experience."

Then she made a liar out of herself by moving up and down with skill and vigor as she took it in to the roots in her tight hot rectum. She leaned forward to brace herself with a palm against his chest while she masturbated her left-over parts with her free hand, saying, "Faith, I'll bet El Cazador in the flesh can't do this any better than me!"

"We'll never know," Captain Gringo laughed. "I'm not going after him to corn-hole his ass. I mean to blow it *off* from the son-of-a-bitch!"

"Och, well, in that case, let's finish right. There are limitations to this approach to paradise. It's a grand new thrill, but I don't think a gorl can come all the way like this."

He didn't answer. His eyes were closed, his teeth gritted, as he exploded in her bounding derrier. She gasped, "Och, I felt that, you dreadful man, and it's left out I feel indeed!"

He rolled her over, leaving his shaft in place as he slid a hand down between them to massage her clit and slide his shaft faster in and out of her confused rear entrance as he kissed her, tongued her, and drove her wild. She wrapped her long black legs around his waist, raised her rump to take it deeper, and shuddered on his shaft in a long throbbing orgasm. She gasped, "Jasus, I'm coming again!" and he said, "That was the general idea."

After that, he did take a short nap. It was early and he couldn't have gotten out of bed, just yet, with a crane.

• • •

They steamed out of San Pedro just after sundown. Aside from Captain Gringo and Gaston, eight other cay men had been dumb enough to volunteer. They were a salt and pepper crew picked from the ruffians, black and white, of the rough little port. But eight men made a corporal's squad and El Cazador had to have more on his side. Aside from personal servants, the notorious Basque planter could probably count on the local rurales in a pinch, and most rurale outposts were company strength. Ergo, if at all possible, they had to hit El Cazador hard and pronto, before he could send for help. The rurales would be based in or near the fishing port of Xcalak. El Cazador's plantation was, say, eight or ten miles out in the jungle from town. Nobody had ever run the four-minute mile, yet, but a messenger could get to the rurales in a quarter hour. El Cazador wouldn't need to do it the hard way if he'd strung a telephone line to town and they said the prick was rich and up-to-date. Okay, the rurales would take a few minutes to saddle up and ride. How much time did they have? Enough to hit and run. Not enough for a siege. Big deal, they didn't have the men and material for a siege in any case. Gaston said they didn't have enough to go anywhere near El Cazador, and Gaston was right. But once they were out on open water Captain Gringo ordered the sails set and set a tack for north by north east. The only bright spot in the kidnapping of Ynez was that they didn't have to worry about cutting across the big bay to drop her off on a safer shore. The girl was already in as much trouble as a girl could get into. The voyage didn't figure to be long, since Ambergris Cay was already rubbing noses with Mexico. There wasn't time to learn or even clearly remember the names of the guys they'd brought along. Pegeen had vouched for them. Captain Gringo had to assume she knew them, whether in the Biblical sense or not. They looked tough. That didn't always mean a hell of a lot.

Captain Gringo had gone west to fight Apache just too late to meet Billy The Kid. But he'd met men who had, and it was generally agreed Bill Bonney, Henry McArthy, or whoever in hell he'd been, had looked like a little sissy. A lot of killers looked like sissies. That was odd, when you thought about it. El Cazador was said to look effeminate, too. Maybe sissy-looking guys thought they had to prove something?

His mixed crew consisted of four whites, three blacks, and a heavy set thug called Smiley who could have said he was either. Smiley seemed a natural leader. So Captain Gringo had Smiley join him and Gaston in the salon as they went over the charts. Captain Gringo pointed out the creek running in behind El Cazador's and the stolen Bilbao plantation. He said, "We'll put in here, then follow the stream inland on foot."

Smiley asked why they didn't just steam up the creek. Captain Gringo said, "Because if I were El Cazador, I'd expect that. He knows we have this vessel and what its capabilities are. A picket posted in the scrub could spot a moving schooner out on the water long before we spotted him. But we can assume any look-outs will be staked out on El Cazador's side of the waterway. So we'll sneak up the other side, make for the Bilbao plantation, and dig in. It might be deserted. It might be being worked by El Cazador's peones. We'll find out when we get there. Either way, it's an opening in the trees we'll be able to find in the dark and, as you see, it's inland from El Cazador's, so he shouldn't expect an attack from that side. Do we have anyone who knows, Smiley?"

Smiley said he'd find out and left. "I passed through years ago when I served with the legion," Gaston said. "I know where the rurale post is, Dick."

"You mean you know where it *was,* say thirty years ago."

"Was it that long? *Merde,* how time flies. But why would they have moved the rurale post, Dick?"

"They may not have, but we have to know for sure. The Diaz dictatorship has made a lot of changes in Mexico since you were swapping shots with Juarez, Gaston."

"That's not fair, I told you I changed sides when I saw the Mexicans were going to win."

"Yeah, yeah, the Siege of Camerone is ancient history. We have to know what's going on in Xcalak tonight."

Smiley came back with a black called Dipper. Dipper said he'd landed in Xcalak a couple of months back and added, "I got out pronto. Them rurales don't like strangers and I don't pass for a Mexican too well. The Indian folk there ain't mean, but them rurales are a caution."

"I've noticed that," Captain Gringo offered. "Take a look at this chart and show me where the rurale post is."

Dipper studied the large scale chart, nodded, and stabbed a finger down on the paper, saying, "Here. Between the jungle and the main town. They's building something else out here on this point. It looked like a low slung fort made outten coral blocks."

Captain Gringo nodded and said, "Probably coastal defenses. You can see how isolated Xcalak is from the rest of Quintana Roo. It's a natural place to run guns in, and when you run a country the way Diaz does, you have to worry about your population getting their hands on guns."

Dipper nodded and confirmed, "That's likely why they acted so surly to strangers. I've heard tell smugglers has used Xcalak as a port of call now and again."

"Yeah, that's probably why Mexico City is taking a tighter hold on the reins. When you were there, did you notice any telegraph or telephone lines, Dipper? I'm particularly worried about it along this stretch of railroad track, here."

Dipper shook his head and said, "Hell, they thinks wax

candles is a new fangled notion in Xcalak. Like I said, the peones is mostly simple barefoot raggedy Indians. I didn't see telephone pole one. Who you fixing to telephone in Xcalak, Captain Gringo?"

"Nobody. The point is that El Cazador doesn't have a telephone, either."

Gaston frowned and said, "I don't like that new fort guarding the harbor, Dick. Coast defense guns make me *très* nervous."

"Shit, we're not about to enter the harbor. We'll be sailing by it, blacked out, well out to sea, in the dark."

"*Oui,* but then, in your madness, you intend to land us up the coast! Don't tell me there's no way to hit a man with an artillery shell, blind, in the jungle. I am an old artillery man. I also know that where one finds a cannon, one finds cannoncers, hein? Add the military garrison to Los Rurales and God knows how many private guns in El Cazador's hip pocket, and tell me how we take them all on at once with eight men!"

The others around the chart table looked concerned too. So Captain Gringo said, "We don't take them all on at once. The coast battery's here, a good three miles from the rurale post. El Cazador's here, miles away from either. He's got maybe two dozen men, period."

"Period hell! He's *expecting* us, and the girl says he's dug in behind thick stone walls, Dick!"

"You want to get out and walk? I know he's expecting us. He's been daring us to come and get him ever since we tangled with him. That's why I'm fucking around with this stupid chart. We have to figure out an approach he won't be expecting!"

"*Merde alors,* there is no such approach! Regardez, he squats like the spider inside four strong walls. He has at least six guns covering each wall. We can attack from the north, south, east, or west. As you say, big deal. As soon as the fighting starts, the military and rurales will come marching to his rescue. There is no way anyone can hope to reduce such a stronghold in less than a day or so of heavy siege."

"Not unless we find a weak spot," Captain Gringo insisted, sliding the chart away, then added, "Like I said, first we sneak inland to the Bilbao spread. Then we do some scouting."

"What if the stolen plantation is occupied, too?"

"Hell, Gaston, you knew we were looking for a fight. What do you want, egg in your beer?"

"*Mais non.* I just wish I could wake up and discover this was all a bad dream! I have followed you through thick and thin, my young and foolish, but this expedition takes the cake. I vote we give it up. I didn't know about that coast artillery when I agreed to this madness!"

Smiley said, "Make that two votes to turn back, Captain. Nobody never said nothing about facing cannon fire!"

Captain Gringo's eyes narrowed dangerously as he said, "Gaston's just farting with his mouth. Nobody gets to vote on this vessel except me. You guys signed on with me, and I'm in command."

Smiley muttered, "That don't sound fair."

So Captain Gringo knocked him on his ass, kicked him to gain his undivided attention, and explained, "It's not supposed to sound fair. This is a military expedition, not a debating society. I shall lead you into green pastures and you shall fear no evil, because I'm as evil a guy as you're likely to meet, and I'm on your side as long as you don't fuck up. Are you goin to fuck up, Smiley?"

Smiley sat up, shook his head, and said, "Hell no, I just had to have it explained to me right, Captain!"

Captain Gringo had planned it so they coasted past Xcalak and put into the black lace mangrove fringe of the peninsula before moonrise. When one of the men asked about leaving a watch aboard the schooner he said, "Skip it. We can't spare enough to guard it properly. So let's just hope nobody finds it 'til we need it again."

"What if they do, Captain?"

"We'll have to steal another boat. All ashore who's going ashore. Dipper, carry this Maxim for me and stick close. I'm taking the point."

All this was easier said than done. The mangrove shore was under maybe a foot of water and a hundred feet of slimy mud. But they made it from the gangplank to solid ground, at last, by watching where they stepped and hanging on to limbs a lot. As expected, the underbrush was thick along the north bank of the salt creek. Captain Gringo led them deeper under the canopy where the shade kept the weeds more reasonable. By now the moon was up, dappling the mucky forest floor with leopard spots of light. There was no trail. That was good. It meant locals walking up and down the stream used the south bank. Captain Gringo started hiking as the others followed, slipping on rotten leaves and cursing softly. He could see they'd been out in the field before. Greenhorns would have cursed louder.

Gaston fell in at his side and started to chatter. Captain Gringo said, "Shut up, I'm counting" and Gaston nodded and kept still. He was an old soldier, too, and knew what the tall American was doing. There were roughly a thousand paces to the military mile. The word came from the Roman word for a thousand, *mille*. The Romans had wanted to know how far they'd marched, too. Miles, a soldier in Latin, was a guy who'd been trained to pace off a consistent military mile. Captain Gringo couldn't see any landmarks but, thanks to the map, he knew how far upstream the Bilbao place was. So a lot of paces and aching legs later he held up a hand to halt his tiny army and said, "Okay, we've passed El Cazador's for sure and we ought to be just past the Bilbao spread he swiped. You guys stay here while I have a look."

Gaston started to follow. Captain Gringo told him to stay put and take command. He didn't know the others as well as Gaston and he was going to feel silly as hell if he came back to find them, his Maxim, and probably the schooner missing.

He bulled through the thicker vegetation along the river bank and the salt water creek, mirror smooth in the moonlight. He saw the far shore was cleared: he'd paced it off right. He couldn't see much of the Bilbao spread, but there were open fields across from him. If he could get across without being eaten alive.

He drew his revolver and held it above his head, to keep it dry, not because it would do him much good if a salt water croc grabbed him. The water was warm as stale tea and came to his waist. He waded across and eased up the far bank, letting most of the water drip from him quietly as he moved on. His boots squished as he moved across an open field, aiming for an inky black mass that had to be the plantation house and out buildings. Apparently the coffee trees Ynez and her husband had planted had been ripped out in favor of some other cash crop. He bent and plucked a spray of whatever the hell it was to look it over later in better light. He was braced for a dog's bark at least as he approached the blacked out house. But there wasn't a sound. So the place was probably deserted. He circled. The plantation house was exposed and indefensible, too. There went a good idea. If he hid his men here, they'd be trapped with open ground all around when the sun rose. They'd have to find a better place. But as long as he was here, he might as well have a look inside. He eased up to the veranda, stepped up on the planks, and cursed as a board squeaked under him. Nothing happened. He moved along the shuttered windows, looking for a way in. He froze again as he heard a muffled sound. It sounded like a woman crying, or trying to. He found a door. It was locked, but the sobbing sounds were coming from just inside. He took a deep breath, hit the door with his shoulder, and busted in, dropping to one knee out of line with the door as he covered the dark interior with his .38. Then he crept toward the source of the sounds, muttered, "Oh, for Pete's sake!" and struck a match.

It was Ynez again. She was dressed, this time, in the same sailor suit she'd last been wearing. But they hadn't shown a bit of originality in the tape and handcuffs. He pulled the tape off her mouth and whispered, "Are we alone?"

"Yes," she said, "but get me out of here! They could be back any minute."

That sounded reasonable. He picked her up, threw her over his shoulder, and ran like hell. On the way she explained how El Cazador had said something about leaving her at her own place as bait, whatever that meant. It didn't make much sense to him, either. He forded the salt creek with her, rejoined the others, and as Gaston picked the locks binding her wrists and ankles, Ynez brought them up to date on her own adventures. She found it a lot more interesting than Captain Gringo. He'd already guessed she'd been brought here by El Cazador and his men. She said, again, she hadn't seen El Cazador in the flesh, but that a couple of goons had shoved her head in a sack and carried her a lot. Gaston said, "Eh bien, so much for the wrists. Let's get the ankles. Why do you suppose they left her there unguarded, Dick? I am overjoyed you found her, and found it so easy to get away as well. But surely they had some point to her abduction, hein?"

"We might have showed up earlier than El Cazador figured. Take a look at what they're growing over there."

Gaston took the crop sample, held it up to the light, and said, "Ahah, opium poppies, non?"

"Yeah, the crop won't mature for a few more weeks, but they've got a hell of a crop of sleepy-sleepy sprouting over there. Is opium growing illegal in Mexico, Gaston?"

"Surely you jest. El Presidente doesn't care what you grow, as long as he gets his cut. Narcotics and alcohol are heavily taxed in all progressive countries, of course. But it's not illegal in Mexico to grow any crop I can think of."

Ynez got to her feet, rubbing her wrists, and said, "It's not fair. They tore out all my nice little coffee trees."

"Yeah," Captain Gringo added, "there's more money in opium. Okay, next question, does that path I noticed behind your house lead to El Cazador's fortified house, Ynez?"

"Not directly, but it leads to a wagon trace through the jungle that does. It's across the railroad tracks and . . ."

"Never mind, just making sure the real world jibes with the chart in my head. Okay, gang, back to the boat. Let's pick 'em up and lay 'em down. We've got some serious moves to make before sunrise."

He detailed two of his men to help Ynez and, of course, he no longer had to count his paces as he led them back toward the coast. So Gaston was able to talk to him as they strode side by side through the jungle. Gaston asked, "Where are we going, Dick? I know you find me a fussy old man, but it's so comforting to know where one is going, hein?"

"I told you," Captain Gringo stated, "we're going back to the schooner."

"Ah? Then, now that you have Ynez back, you are having second thoughts about the serious nature of this dispute with El Cazador?"

"Shit, I haven't even started with El Cazador. I mean to fix El Cazador's wagon for keeps!"

"I was afraid you'd say that. But are we not passing

his private fort about now? I, too, read maps. I would say it is almost directly across the salt creek from here, non?"

"You're right. And if we tried to hit them from this direction they'd chop hell out of us."

"True, but is it any safer to attack stout stone walls from the west?"

"Nope. I've convinced myself there has to be a better way."

"I'm so happy for you. But what other way is there, Dick? El Cazador is expecting us from all four directions, non?"

"Sure, that's why we're going to hit in a way nobody could possibly expect us to. Pick 'em up and lay 'em down. Like I said, I'm in a hurry."

Captain Gringo got his people back aboard the schooner, told Ynez to go below where she'd be safe, and spent the next few minutes getting well off shore under steam power with the sails furled. Then he set a course due south, told Dipper to hold her that way, and took Gaston and Smiley aside to explain his plan. They both seemed surprised as hell, but Gaston said, "*Parbleu*! It works! It must be the last thing El Cazador would expect us to try, since I never even considered it and I, as you know, am a military genius!"

"I must be a military genius, too!" Smiley laughed. "I can see it working, and once you point it out, it's so simple I'm kicking myself for not thinking of it myself! This time you don't have to beat me up, Captain. I'm with you. You're starting to make sense for a change!"

Captain Gringo's plan was childishly simple. So simple that, like all really good military plans, the other side had no defenses planned to counter it. One only sets up defenses against the expected.

They steamed boldly into the port of Xcalak. When a search light winked on from the low coral walls of the small coastal defense installation, Captain Gringo nudged Dipper, at the helm, and said, "Swing her bows and steam for that landing by the gate of the fort."

Dipper did as he was told, but said, "I hopes you know what you're doing, Captain! We're right under their guns, and getting closer by the cotton-picking minute!"

"I know what I'm doing. They don't," Captain Gringo said. "This schooner sails from this port on a regular basis and it's easy to recognize. As for the guns, look again. That installation's not meant to fire point blank at boats in the harbor. There are no embrasures in those walls. Any guns inside are meant to lob shells long distance, *over* the walls."

Before his helmsman could comment further, Captain Gringo moved forward, warning the men crouched in the cockpit and on the seaward side of the cabin to keep out of sight and take their lead from him. He joined Gaston near the foremast, where the machinegun was loaded and armed but under a tarp atop the cabin. Gaston pointed shoreward with his chin to observe, "So far, so good, but they certainly seem trusting. You must have been right about El Cazador not reporting the theft of his schooner to his friends in high places."

"I know the Mexican authorities don't know we're not working for El Cazador, now. They'd be shooting at us if they even considered we were pirates."

Gaston blanched and asked, "You know it *now*, not *before*?"

"We had to take the chance. But don't look so wounded. I had a pretty good idea El Cazador never reported us grabbing the tub. It was the only way we could get here, and El Cazador's invited us to come more than once, so what the hell."

Dipper reversed the screw as they approached the landing and the schooner was moving dead slow when its fenders nudged the dock. Smiley leaped ashore with the hauser and made it fast. An N.C.O. in Mexican navy kit strolled out through the open gate, calling, "Hey, for why are you boys tying up here?"

Smiley didn't speak good Spanish and he'd already shown himself not to be a heavy thinker. He drew his pistol and blasted the Mexican coming out of the fort. Naturally a fusilade of hot lead came out of the fort, too, and that was the end of Smiley.

Gaston cursed as Smiley went down, riddled from head to toe, but Captain Gringo looked at the bright side while he tore the tarp off the Maxim. As they chopped the already dead Smiley to ground meat on the dock, the chumps were giving their positions away, and not shooting at anyone else!

Before they could, Captain Gringo opened up with the machinegun, traversing along the castilated slots atop the coral wall while the others, opening up with their Winchesters, concentrated on muzzle flashes from the few loop holes lower down.

By the time he'd used up one belt of ammo in the moonlit fire fight, the dense cloud of gunsmoke enveloping both sides was causing more confusion than casualties. So Captain Gringo snapped in a fresh belt and, with it trailing behind him like a lashing brass dragon's tail, he leaped ashore, tore down through the open gate, and wound up in the dark center of the installation before any of the artillerymen manning the walls could shoot or even notice him.

He could see them, though. They were outlined against the sky and rising moonlit gunsmoke, so he simply braced the Maxim on his hip and opened fire as he made a slow and not too graceful ballerina twirl, hosing hot lead. Most of the defenders had bunched above the gate. So he sent most of the rounds their way after brushing the whole parapet free of pests smart enough to be guarding the other loop holes. The results were grisly even for machinegun fire. The slugs ripped through the men, hit the brittle coral blocks, and bounced back to mangle anyone still on his feet. The shattered coral fragments did a job on them too.

By the time he'd used most of the belt, Captain Gringo ran out of targets and squinted through the smoke around him to get his bearings. In the lousy light he could just make out the bulky outlines of the coast defense gun squatting near the open center of the fortification. Black squares against the barely visible coral all around indicated that the quarters and other installations needing a roof had been built into the thick walls. He thought of busting some glass with his last rounds, remembered artillery shells had to have some damned place in here, and decided he'd better not. A weak voice was sobbing, "Cuartel! Cuartel! Por favor cuartel!" when he noticed his own guys outside had ceased fire. Then a door opened and a fat officer dashed out, firing wildly from the hip. So Captain Gringo emptied the belt-end into him, rolling him up into a ball of bloody hash, and growled, "What's the matter with you, didn't you hear the other guys giving up?"

Gaston called out, "Dick?" and he yelled, "Over here. Report!"

"One casualty. That black called Trinidad caught a lucky round with his eyebrow. What's the situation in here?"

Captain Gringo could make out others with Gaston in the smoke now, so he said, "Don't know. I want a mop-up detail to sweep through the rooms built into the walls. Have somebody do what they can for the wounded up there who've given up."

"Dick, we have no medicine or bandages."

"I know. Disarm the ones who look like they might

get well on their own and put the others out of their misery. I'll be right back."

He placed the machinegun on the ground, dog-trotted back out to the schooner and leaped back aboard to get more ammo. When he heard pounding he called down an air vent, "Sit tight, Doll. You're safer there than anywhere I can think of right now!"

"Dick," Ynez yelled back, "I'm locked in this cabin! I can't get out!"

He yelled, "Yeah, that's why I locked you in. Don't worry, you're below the water line if you hit the deck, so do that, if you notice any bullets coming through the planking. The tub can't sink enough to matter in these shallows. Hang in there. Can't talk now."

She was cussing him a blue streak as he leaped back ashore, grinning. He considered making her possibly more secure inside the fortifications, but he was pressed for time and didn't intend to stay there long. When he rejoined Gaston near the big gun, the smoke had cleared and he could see more detail in the bright moonlight. The solodad gun was the only one they'd installed, but it made up for it by being a six-incher. Gaston said, "About the Mexicans . . . I made the mistake of telling Dipper to look after them and he was Trinidad's side kick, so . . ."

"Never mind the petty details. Are you ready to fire that cannon?"

"I will be in a moment. I detailed some of the boys to fetch me some shells from the casement over there."

Captain Gringo took the folded chart out of his shirt front and gave it to Gaston, saying, "Okay, I'm mounting the Maxim above the gate to keep people from bothering you while you take out the three targets I've marked. Can do?"

"*Mais oui*, I am an old artillery man and this gun has more than enough range. But I don't understand why you want me to huff and puff at the Bilbao plantation as well.

The rurale post and that castle of El Cazador make sense. But won't Ynez be annoyed if we break all her windows?"

"There's no way she'll ever to be able to reclaim the land now, and she said some of the gang was using the house. Don't argue about it. That rurale post isn't all that far and we took this place sort of noisy!"

He picked up the Maxim, lugged it up a nearby stone stairway to the top of the parapet, and moved over above the gate. He propped the warm barrel in a slot dominating the only approach from the town across the harbor and lit a smoke to see what he could see. Nothing much seemed to be happening. The lights were on in the little fishing village. So he assumed everyone was up. The schooner below lay to his right, just out of the way if he wanted to fire along the waterside path from town. But the path lay deserted in the silvery moonlight.

He found this no big mystery. He knew if he were a rurale officer and all hell broke loose in the night, he'd fort up inside his outpost and wait for some light on the subject, too. Los Rurales might put out a few scouts. Most would be at the station on the far side of town until dawn at least.

He winced and almost bit off his cigar at the roots when Gaston fired the big gun behind him. It felt like a six-inch shell was whizzing up his spine. But he forgave Gaston. The old Frenchman was good. Another shell followed the first while the air was still tingling and he knew Gaston was a crack shot with big guns. Gaston had the long-range coastal defense gun aimed almost straight up, so as to lob the shells like mortar rounds. Gaston could drop a mortar round in a barrel if he wanted to show off. At this moderately longer range, some few shells were bound to miss. But Gaston was firing a mess of them, so what the hell.

He heard the distant summer thunder of the first shells

landing behind the village across the way, and saw the treetops outlined in the winking orange flashes of exploding H.E. Then the light stayed on and started spreading. Something was on fire over that way and burning good. He turned and yelled down, "You got the rurales! Dust off Target Two!"

The big gun went off in his face. He swore and turned his back on it, covering his ears with cupped palms. It didn't help a lot. His head was ringing like a kicked spitoon. But he had to stay up here and guard the approaches. He had a good view, too. Off to the north, he saw the flashes of Gaston's exploding shells. Standing vegetation didn't burn well in this humidity, so that other orange glow in the sky meant Gaston was on target again. He didn't have to tell Gaston when to change targets. The sly old legionnaire knew by instinct just how many rounds it took to take out a baby fort. Captain Gringo saw brighter air bursts above the jungle to the north and grinned. Gaston had a nasty imagination. He'd fused the last rounds short, to dust the shattered ruins of the thick walled casa with shrapnel. There would probably be a few survivors. There were always a few survivors, but anyone who lived through one of Gaston's barrages tended to crawl in a hole and stay there a while.

The big gun fell silent for the time it took Gaston to traverse and elevate to a new target. Then he opened up again and lobbed the last of the ammo on hand down on the house Captain Gringo had found Ynez alone in. Gaston had allowed for the relative strength of each target's walls in dividing the shells on hand. So after dropping a half dozen on or damned close to the last house on his list, Gaston was out of ammo.

He joined Captain Gringo on the parapet, gazed out in satisfaction at the three separate conflagrations on the horizon, and said, "Eh bein. To be certain one would have to send out patrols. But to stay here that long could be injurious to one's health, hein? We have rescued the girl and if El Cazador lived through all that, I doubt he will ask us for a rematch in the near future. Why don't we get back aboard our *très* jolly pirate ship and be on our way?"

"Because, for one thing," Captain Gringo answered, "it's a pirate ship. These waters are lousy with gunboats and some of them have wireless sets. El Cazador's tub is too well known and those dark sails are distinctive."

"Agreed, but what else did you have in mind?"

"New sails, of course. Xcalak is a fishing village. They're sure to have a sail loft that can fit us out with plain canvas."

"*Sacre,* you are going into town?"

"No. The town ought to come to us any minute. It's almost dawn."

He was right. The alcalde and priest of Xcalak didn't wait until full daylight before they came out along the pathway with a small delegation under a waving white flag. Captain Gringo hailed them closer. They stopped at rifle range, the priest coming forward, holding the flag. When he was within earshot he stopped and called out, "We surrender, Señor Pirator! We have no policia or soldados for to protect us, now. My people are simple pobrecitos. They have no treasure. But I will give you the plate from my church if you will not abuse the women of Xcalak!"

"We're not pirates, Padre," Captain Gringo called back. "We're not after money and your women are safe."

"I thank God as well as you, señor. But if you are not pirates, for why have you killed all the policia and soldados?"

"They caught me in a bad mood. I do want some things from your villagers, though. Get the alcalde out here."

"*Por favor,* he is afraid, señor."

"All right, Padre. You can tell him what I want. Tell

him I'll pay for a suit of fresh sails for that schooner, there, and we could use a few baskets of fresh produce and a barrel of cerveza."

The townspeople were delighted with the easy terms. So by early morning Captain Gringo and his cutthroat crew were sailing down the coast again with new sails as they rationed out the fairly good home brew. Just before leaving, they'd learned from excited peones from the tall timber that Gaston's shells had done a job on all three targets. Nobody had been seen alive around the cratered ruins of any of them.

As Captain Gringo lounged in the cockpit with Dipper manning the helm, a lookout aloft, and the others sipping cerveza here and there, Gaston came up from below to join him, asking, "What have you done with the key to that cabin you locked Ynez in, Dick? She's pounding like a maniac and I wasn't able to let her out."

Captain Gringo said, "I don't want you to let her out. She *is* a maniac. Jesus, haven't you figured it out yet?"

Gaston sat beside him with a puzzled frown and asked what the hell he was talking about. So Captain Gringo said, "Ynez is El Cazador. When we get back to Ambergris Cay, we'll work out some way for Pegeen O'Hara and the boyos to turn her over to the British authorities for the reward. We owe old Pegeen, remember?"

Gaston's jaw dropped. Then he shook his head and said, "You're drunk! Ynez is a *woman*!"

"Yeah, a great lay, too. That's why everybody thought El Cazador was a swish. Ynez is nutty as a fruit cake, but no matter how she tried to pass for a man she just couldn't manage to screw dames."

"*Merde alors,* I am *très* confused, I thought . . ."

"I know what you thought. I did, too, until I started putting lots of odd twos and twos together. Would it help if I started at the beginning?"

"I certainly wish you would."

"Okay, once upon a time, in far off Spain, a respectable Basque family whose name escapes me, had a black sheep. You were right that Montalban is a place, not a family name. According to the Spanish Inquisition, Montalban was the center of witchcraft and devil worship in the dark ages. I don't know if the inquisition was on to something or if Ynez just read too much. Anyway, she grew up mean and crazy. She must have done something awful and had to leave in a hurry, dressed as a man. She's not that flat chested, but she's tall for a Latin woman and the first time I met her I thought she wore a wig. With close cropped hair, a mannish stride, and a pretty good gun hand, she had no trouble convincing people she was a sissy-looking guy. She left Spain with money, either stolen or given by relations to get her out of their hair. She came to Quintana Roo and became a planter, growing opium for fun and profit. Her plantation was in a remote area. So she profited even more by not paying taxes to the Mexican government. She bullied and intimidated the locals by convincing them she was some sort of sadistic grandee when she used anyone who didn't jump when she said froggy for target practice. The local rurales thought she was their kind of guy. She bribed them a little and entertained them a lot. But remember, she was dealing with dedicated bully boys who would have turned on her had they even suspected she was a woman, or worse yet, a fairy!"

"I know the macho mentality, Dick, but the hunting trips to Africa, the English girl she married, it's all so utterly mad!"

"Look, I just told you she was *nuts*! She really enjoyed blood and slaughter and, as we guessed, she hunted partly for profit as well. Opium growing doesn't take a lot of effort when you have peones doing all the work. Maybe someone she knew was getting suspicious of the apparently celibate life their boon companion led. Don't try to figure out the details of a lunatic's thought processes. Suffice it to say, she took a trip to let things cool off. She got in trouble with the Brits by indulging herself in mistreating natives more than even Victoria approved. So she had to come back, pronto. But she was afraid they were still making cracks about the way El Cazador walked. Passing as a handsome young man, she met Morgana in London, fed the English fortune hunting girl a line of shit about being a rich planter, and brought Morgana home as her wife. That satisfied the local bully boys, but of course it didn't satisfy Morgana. That's why when we met her she'd just run away from what she thought was her sadistic celibate husband. Ynez didn't know I'd had a chance to get to know Morgana pretty good. El Cazador was told the runaway girl died in that fire, remember?"

"*Oui,* but what *could* the English girl have told you, that her husband was another girl?"

"No, Morgana never saw El Cazador with his pants off. But she did describe their plantation. She said they had no neighbors, other than military, and she never mentioned it having stone walls like a castle. I'd forgotten that 'til last night, when we were planning to attack El Cazador's stronghold. That fortification out in the jungle wasn't El Cazador's place. The so-called Bilbao plantation was."

"Then who the devil *did* live in that castle, and where was the real Bilbao plantation?"

"Let's take it in reverse to keep it simple. There was no real Bilbao plantation. Nobody named Bilbao ever came to Mexico. Ynez made all that up because she had to be *somebody* when she was conning me, dressed as a woman. That walled outpost was the point of her whole shell game. It was a federale post. A new one. You see, she had the local rurales in her hip pocket. So she was paying no taxes to Mexico City. But El Presidente Diaz collects a healthy duty on narcotics indeed. And, for the same reasons they built that new coastal defense fort we shot up, the federales decided to garrison more troops along the only railroad track in the area."

"*Parbleu*! You mean we shot up an *army garrison* stationed in Target Two?"

"Why not? They'd have shot *us*, right? Never miss the chance to take a leak or shoot anybody working for Diaz. Do you want me to explain or don't you?"

"I wish you would. What connection did the army have with El Cazador?"

"They complicated his/her life. Like I said, Ynez, posing as El Cazador, had the rurales bribed. She probably could have bribed the federales. But if you're going to bribe *everybody*, you may as well pay the damned taxes, and she was ever a willful child. She thought pretty good on her feet, too. When Morgana ran away, Ynez had to chase her as a macho Latin hubby would be expected to. So they were closing in on Morgana when the English girl lucked on to us and we helped her. Ynez didn't know how much we helped her, but she knew who we were and we were just what the doctor ordered for a crazy lady with pesky new neighbors. Not even El Cazador could shoot up a federale garrison, so she started all that razzle-dazzle to get us to go up there and start a guerrilla war with the army. She didn't give a shit who won. She just wanted the soldados too busy to bother her while she harvested a final crop of opium before moving on to greener pastures, see?"

"*Sacre bleu,* I am beginning to. As El Cazador she taunted and dared to get you to come north. As the poor Basque widow she offered other inducements."

"Yeah, her inducements were pretty good. I guess a girl gets hard up, pretending to be a man most of the time. She pretended good, both ways. Now that I look back, I feel kind of dumb when I consider how many times I seemed to be rescuing her from herself."

"Wait, let me be smart, too," Gaston laughed. "That

machinegun ambush in the alley was a ruse to convince you she was what she seemed: a fellow victim of the notorious El Cazador, no?"

"Yeah, the first belt they fired at us was loaded with blanks. I probably upset her by shooting her crew. That wasn't the plan. She just wanted me to trust her and to get my hands on a machinegun."

"Eh bien, I would want the notorious Captain Gringo armed with a Maxim when I sent him after my real enemies, too. But the times you rescued her, chained hand and foot . . ."

"Hell, that was easy. I got to wondering about that, the second time she pulled it. The first time El Cazador kidnapped her, she hadn't planned on being kidnapped. She was just on her yacht, alone save for one deck hand, when we surprised her by grabbing it. She ran below, pasted tape over her own mouth, and snapped those cuffs on. She probably had cuffs handy because she was a bounty hunter on the side and sometimes you get more returning a prisoner alive. Anyway, she let us find her as El Cazador's prisoner in his hold. She must have been scared skinny. She sure screwed like she wanted to make friends. We steamed out with her alone. But she was a quick thinker. She went along with the gag when she saw we were playing into her hands."

"But the second kidnapping?"

"Easy. El Cazador couldn't make any moves while he was palling around with us as my girl. So as soon as she had the chance, she killed Cockpit Calvin, tossed the two heads to the crabs, and just walked ashore with a rifle held down at her side. And who looks? The north end of Ambergris Cay is a short paddle from the mainland. So she just kept walking. Like a chump, I followed to rescue her some more. She didn't want to be rescued, so she pinned me down in the scrub with pretty good rifle fire. I say pretty good because she was careful not to kill me.

She still needed my services even if she didn't want to sleep with me any more. Do you need the rest of it?"

Gaston shook his head and said, "Non, I can put it together from when we left San Pedro to save the poor maiden in distress. When she heard you scouting her real plantation she simply repeated the droll business with the tape and handcuffs, you rescued her, and we all know what transpired from there on. Does she know, yet, that we are on to her and what we intend for El Cazador?"

Captain Gringo shrugged and said, "I imagine she must, from the way she's been trying to bust out of that cabin since I locked her in it."

"How droll," Gaston chuckled. "But are you sure she is secure down there, Dick? We know she is *très diabolique* and if she can get her treacherous hands on anything she could use to jimmy the door . . ."

"She won't. I made sure there was nothing in the cabin but the bunk and looked under the mattress as well."

"*Eh bien,* but who knows what she might have under her clothes?"

"What clothes? I left her in there stark naked."

"You stripped the poor child before locking her in?"

"Not exactly; I paid her a visit just before we steamed into Xcalak. She was anxious to stay in good with me. So naturally I had no trouble getting in her good. You can't screw a lady wearing sailor pants. So I asked her to take off the pants and shirt and she did. It was dark and I told her I had business topside. So after we tore off a quicky, I rolled off, grabbed her duds on the fly, and locked the door before she'd even had a chance to say adios. We'll give her something to wear when we take her ashore in San Pedro, if she behaves herself. At the moment she's locked in bare ass. I doubt even El Cazador could pick a lock with a fingernail, right?"

"Your ingenuity astounds me! Do you mean to tell me you could still get it up for her, knowing she was the murderous El Cazador? I don't think even I would wish to fuck a creature like that!"

"Why not? She'd sure fucked *me* a lot, both ways."

When they got back to San Pedro, Captain Gringo went below with a man's shirt in one hand and his .38 in the other. He unlocked the cabin door and found Ynez seated naked on the bunk. By the light from the small porthole, her eyes looked wild as those of a trapped wolf. But she smiled and leaned back, opening her thighs invitingly. He tossed the shirt at her and said, "Put this on. I can't think of a way I haven't had you and, frankly, the bloom is off the rose, *El Cazador*. Or should I call you *La Cazadora?*"

She sat up straighter, sighed, and said, "So you know. What happens now? Are you going to kill me, Darling?"

"I'm not your *Darling* and I'm going to let the British government do whatever they like to you after we turn you over to them. I don't know if they still hang dames or not. Put on that shirt."

She didn't. She fell to her naked knees at his feet and sobbed, "No, not *that*! You don't understand! The British will turn me over to *Spain* and the Spanish execute by slow strangulation!"

"Yeah. I've heard of La Garrota. You sure have led an active life, Doll. What are you wanted for in Spain? Never mind, I can guess. Come on, get dressed, I'm taking you ashore."

"Please, Dick, in the name of God, I'll do anything you want, but don't let them strangle me!"

"Sorry, Kiddo. We've exhausted all the positions I can think of and you must have known the penalty for murder in your own country before you became such a tomboy."

She rolled over on her hands and knees, presenting her

upthrust rump submissively. He grimaced and said, "Let's go. Another lady already suggested I try that with El Cazador, but somehow the opportunity just doesn't appeal to me. You want to walk down the gangplank like a lady or do I carry you kicking and screaming?"

She cursed him in her own mysterious lingo as she crawled to the bunk, put on the loose shirt, and rose in her bare feet. He ushered her out with his .38 and marched her ashore. A crowd had gathered on the pier. Ynez looked not unattractive with her long shapely legs exposed like that, but Cockpit Calvin had had friends on the cay and they cursed her good as Captain Gringo and his crew frog marched her to Pegeen O'Hara's.

Pegeen cursed her, too, and told one of her lady wrestlers, the black one, to lock Ynez in the liquor locker for now. As the large black girl led Ynez out back, Pegeen said a mailboat from the mainland was due any time now. Meanwhile, her help could take care of her other customers and she wanted to take care of Captain Gringo. That sounded reasonable. Despite his distaste for the treacherous Ynez, the Basque beauty's nude temptations had aroused his appetite for nicer girls, and Pegeen was nice indeed.

He left Gaston in charge out front and followed the junoesque black Irishwoman back to her velvet-lined love nest. He started to retell her about the reward as Pegeen shed her clothes. Pegeen turned, plastered her naked body against him, and sighed, "Och, the divvel take the damned auld reward. You know what I really want, Richard Walker of the mighty tool!"

He wanted her, too. But as he started to undress they heard the sound of screams and breaking glass!

He said, "Hold that thought!" and ran to find out what the hell was going on.

When he got to the open door of the cinder block liquor locker and elbowed some earlier arrivals out of the way, he encountered one hell of a fight. He saw no reason to butt in, either, for it looked dangerous. The desperate Ynez had grabbed a bottle from the racks, smashed it, and slashed the husky black lady wrestler with it, ripping her cotton shift down the front and exposing lots of bleeding black flesh. But that had only been the beginning. By the time Captain Gringo arrived, the big negress had Ynez by the throat and flat on her back with her naked legs flailing desperately. Gaston joined Captain Gringo, saw what was going on, and said, conversationally, "I'll bet on the black one."

"No bet," Captain Gringo said. "Do you think we ought to stop them?"

"But why? They were only going to strangle her in Spain in any case and the lady on top has as good a reason, non?" Captain Gringo made a wry face.

The enraged negress was slashed shallow but slashed a lot. Her blood dripped all over Ynez's chest and face as those big black hands gripped tighter and tighter around her throat. The Basque girl's face was blue where it wasn't spattered with blood, and her naked groin was exposed so everyone could see the awsome contractions and dilations of her body openings down there. Captain Gringo said, "I can't watch this." But as he stepped through the door to end the one-sided struggle, Ynez farted, defecated, urinated, and went very very limp. The tall American put a gentle hand on the muscular shoulder of the negress and said, softly, "Come on, we've got to get you cleaned up."

"I'll kill her!" the negress muttered, numbly adding, "She *cut* me! She cut me good and I means to kill her, mon!"

"You already have. She's dead and you're bleeding like a stuck pig. Come on, let me help you to your feet."

The lady wrestler gave Ynez's neck another good squeeze, let go, gave a funny little sigh, and started to pass out. Captain Gringo caught her under the arms and lifted her gently off Ynez to lay her comfortably on her own back. Pegeen came in, wrapped in her kimono, and gasped, "Jasus, what happened here! Never mind, I've eyes to see! Somebody fetch me medical kit from the far end of the bar!"

Nobody paid much attention to Ynez until Pegeen had cleaned and taped the glass cuts of her injured employee. The black girl was starting to regain consciousness as others picked her up to carry her to her own quarters. Pegeen got to her feet, turned to stare down at Ynez, and said, "Jasus, what a mess! I'll have to have this floor mopped down with lye water as soon as we bury the slut!"

"Don't do that," Captain Gringo said. "Don't you have an ice house?"

"Of course I have an ice house, but why on earth would I want to put the likes of her on ice?"

"You said the mailboat will arrive any time now. Don't you want to collect the reward on El Cazador, Pegeen?"

"I would that, but as you see she's dead, and a cunt besides!"

"The reward was for dead or alive. I can't appear at the Governor's Mansion for you, but some of my crewmen aren't wanted by the law and they can back you when you explain El Cazador was really a woman. The governments of both Britain and Spain must have photos or other ways to identify that face, if you can only preserve her features a little while."

Pegeen brightened and agreed, "Sure and I'll have her stuffed if it means collecting the price on her ugly head!"

Captain Gringo didn't argue. Actually, old Ynez did look sort of ugly right now. She'd been pretty enough, alive, but nobody looked their best with their eyes bulging and their tongue sticking out like that. It was odd—she'd died in exactly the same fashion she'd dreaded so. La Garrotta couldn't have done it any better. Yet, had she been willing to take her chances with less rough justice, it seemed unlikely even a stern Spanish court would have condemned her to any kind of death. Spain recognized insanity as a defense, too.

Pegeen ordered her hired help to put Ynez on ice and clean up the mess. Then she led Captain Gringo to her own quarters, shut the door firmly, and said, "As I was saying before we was so rudely interrupted, I've got a better way to spend the cool of morning than staring at the dead and injured. But now that I've had a better look at that white girl's legs, I think I may have a bone to pick with you!"

He reached down to unfasten her sash as he grinned and said, "Honey, you can pick my bone all you want. It's at your complete disposal."

She slipped out of the kimono with a smile and flopped across the red velvet spread invitingly. But as he took off his own clothes, Pegeen said, "Fess up, now. I know how you men are when it comes to a well-turned ankle, and you had more than that captive's ankles at your complete disposal. I know women, too. She must have offered all she had to you if only you would let her go, right?"

He laughed and climbed on the bed with her, naked, as he soothed, "Hell, I didn't let her go, did I?" Then he took the ebony Pegeen in his arms and kissed her. She returned his kisses warmly, but like many a woman, she seemed to have a one-track mind once her curiosity was aroused. As he started fondling her, Pegeen demanded, "Weren't you even tempted?"

He nuzzled her neck as he slid his hand down between her dark thighs and answered, "Hell, no, I knew you'd be waiting for me here."

"Och, cut your blarney and . . . would you rub a little higher? I said I know how you men are. Faith, I'll bet you had your way with that other woman, evil as she might have been."

He rolled atop her, got it into position, and thrust home hard.

Pegeen's eyes opened wide as she gasped, "Och, Jasus! Not so deep at first! Let a gorl get used to that murtherous weapon before you really use it on her!"

But he had a point to make, and making it was easy with such a nicely built partner. So he started pounding and Pegeen started responding as she smiled radiantly up at him and gushed, "Och, I see I wronged you, Darling. For no man of mortal clay could be so passionate if he'd been with another woman within at least a month!"

They were too busy to talk about it anymore for a long sweet time. But then, after she'd come a couple of times, Pegeen opened her eyes with a puzzled little frown and said, "Wait a minute. You had *me* in this very bed not twenty-four hours ago!"

"What can I tell you?" he laughed. "It's a gift, I guess."

She arched her back and crooned, "It is, and I'm enjoying it. But aren't you getting tired, darling? Do you want me to get on top?"

"Later. We've got lots of time and I'm coming."

"Och, Jasus, so you are, and would you mind if I came along?"

That was the end of her suspicions. For as she later observed, she saw no way he could be such a grand lover this morning if he'd so much as looked at another woman since the last time they'd made love. They made love for a couple of hours, then fell asleep in each other's arms. He'd intended to spend the whole day in bed with Pegeen: she was willing and God knew he deserved it. But Gaston came to the door around two in the afternoon and gave his sneaky secret rap.

Pegeen was asleep, so he left her that way as he slipped on his pants and opened the door a crack for Gaston. Gaston said, "Get the rest of it on. We have a problem."

Captain Gringo knew the only time Gaston didn't beat around the bush was when things were desperate. So he quickly climbed into his duds and .38 and joined Gaston out in the dark hallway, asking what was up.

Gaston said, "A boat just pulled into the harbor. It was not the mailboat we were expecting. Your old chum, Greystoke, has landed on this cay. It gets worse. Greystoke's not alone. He has a squad of Royal Marines with him!"

"I get the message. Back door?"

"Non! I just spotted a marine out back in the palmettos. I do not think he is taking a piss!"

The two soldiers of fortune headed out to the main room of the saloon. Then they froze in place. Greystoke of British Intelligence was enjoying a drink at the bar with another man in the officer's tropical kit of Her Majesty's Marines. Two enlisted marines stood by the door, either because they were not allowed to drink with their superiors or to keep anyone from leaving. Greystoke had seen them. So Captain Gringo nodded and walked over to him, Gaston trailing, uncertain of the form. Greystoke nodded back and said, "Ah, there you are, Walker. I'd introduce you to my drinking companions, but that would mean they'd have to arrest you, what?"

Captain Gringo didn't answer. The officer picked up his highball and moved to a table out of earshot. It was nice to see Greystoke had him so well trained. The sardonic Britisher signaled the barkeep. Nobody else was in the joint. Greystoke said, "Let me buy you chaps a drink. I'm so glad I didn't have to come looking for you. Saves a lot of bother and anxiety, what?"

"You knew we were here?"

"Spotted El Cazador's yacht out front as we were passing. Nice trick with the sails, but I'm paid to notice details. We just heard about your show to the north. Jolly good. We'll see your chums, here, get the reward. What are we drinking, chaps?"

The two soldiers of fortune ordered ale. This was a lousy time to get drunk. As the barkeep served them, Captain Gringo said, "I just finished playing lots of cat and mouse with an expert. What's the story, Greystoke?"

"That's up to you," the spy master replied, with a steely glitter in his eyes that belied his friendly tone as he explained. "I told you the last time we met that I had some unfinished business up this way. You turned me down. That wasn't very friendly."

"Maybe I was a little hasty?"

"Quite so. But never mind, I need a little help up Yucatan way. It's the rough sort of business you chaps are so good at."

"Jesus, Greystoke, we just came from Mexico after smoking up a lot of guys!"

"They shouldn't expect you back so soon, then, what? Of course, if you'd rather face a British court than a few hundred Mexicans . . ."

"Tell me about it," said Captain Gringo.

Gaston gulped his beer and muttered, "*Sacre bleu,* here we go again!"